Hatred towards Love

Hypocrisy & Reality
Book: 6

fiction
by
'Videh' Arvind Kumar

1969 to 1970
(a novel)
(class 7th)
(*Inaayatpur*)

Dedication

Hatred towards Love
(Hypocrisy & Reality:
Book 6)

Dedicated to those innocent lasses who in their school days loved me passionately without caring for what the other class-fellows felt about their actions, and who by their exalted valuation of me, catapulted me to the realm of a celebrity or a child prodigy!

Table of Contents

Dedication 2

Table of Contents 3

Copyright 4

Preface 5

Transcripts of *Hindee* letters and *maatraas* 6

1. Cycle Turns Full Circle.............. 7

2. Father's Sins and Libel 11

3. Peasants Don't Know How To Plough The Fields 16

4. Onslaught Of Nymphs 18

5. Hell-fire Of Carnal Passions..... 21

6. Love's Labour Lost 25

7. Curse of Venus.................... 27

8. Lunar Eclipse In The Mart..... 31

9. Recompense For Oblations 35

10. Another Lady Love From My Previous Birth...................... 38

11. Intense Desire Of Roopwatee Fulfilled............................ 43

12. I Beat A Bully With Scale In The Class 47

13. Never Go Near The Devils..... 49

14. Dwarfism Of Masters 54

15. Rustic Love Affairs 60

16. Manly shame.................... 63

17. Mumrejpur Teacher Manhandled 65

18. Father Departs To Ajmer....... 68

19. Gaandhee's Centenary: My Tryst With His Truth!..................... 72

20. My Trip To Aleegarh And Gaandhee Jayantee 80

21. Towards The Yogaasans 83

22. Yogmudraa and Experience Of Nothingness, i.e. Absolute Void....... 85

23. My Two Year Old Sister Falls Sick 88

24. Birth Of A Brother And Calamitous Portents.................. 90

25. Pandit Boy Thrashes Me Unprovoked Before The Guests, My Cousins.............................. 95

26. Visit Of VIP Guest From Somnaa and My Neglectful Attitude Towards Him 97

27. School Result And New Summits of Glory 101

English Books by 'Videh' 104

'विदेह' रचित हिंदी ग्रंथ 108

लेखक-परिचय 111

About the Author.................. 112

Copyright

Preface

'Hatred towards Love', the sixth volume in the fiction series 'Hypocrisy & Reality' furthers the journey of the protagonist into the world where to his amusement he found himself catapulted into the realm of a celebrity or at least a child prodigy as far as the small rural catchment area was concerned. By virtue of his giftedness in the realm of studies and his bewitching countenance, the classmates, especially, the lasses of her age could not help restraining themselves from loving him; and they did it overtly, without caring for the opinions and feelings of other class-fellows. Though the protagonist wallowed in the faulty ideology that having any truck with fair sex was anathema and a great sin which could not be washed away in later life. There were others, the fellow lads, who did not care for such convictions and believed in free-style mingling with the girls and boys and had no inhibitions as regards sexual conduct or misconduct; it was all the same for them. However, the protagonist could not bring himself upto that level of thinking, and his resolve not to have any connection or conversation with the fellow beauties of the class paradoxically intensified the intensity of affection of girls towards him. He had an apprehension that had he succumbed to the inducements of the girls and toed their line, he would not have been that much liked by the same girls. Such is the attribute of love! The farther you go away from one, the more attractive you become for the one!

However, that was not the only phenomenon taking place during this period; there were other umpteen number of interesting developments in the journey of life of the protagonist which would find place in this volume.

कुणाल-जातक-कथा से:-

दिव्यखिड्डरतियो च नन्दने, चक्कवत्तिचरितञ्च मानुसे।
नासयन्ति पमदा पमादिनम्, दुग्गतिञ्च पटिपादयन्ति नं।।
(ख्रियाँ प्रमादियों की नंदन वन की दिव्य क्रीड़ा युक्त रति तथा मनुष्य लोक में चक्रवर्ती चरित का नाश कर देती हैं और उनकी दुर्गति का कारण होती हैं।)

दिव्यखिड्डरतियो च दुल्लभा, चक्कवत्तिचरितञ्च मानुसे।
सोण्णब्यह्मनिलया च अच्छरा, ये चरन्ति पमदाहनत्थिका।।
(जो ख्रियों के प्रति अनासक्त रहते हैं उन्हें दिव्य क्रीड़ा रति भी दुर्लभ नहीं और मनुष्य लोक में चक्रवर्ती राज्य भी दुर्लभ नहीं, तथा स्वर्णमय विमानों में रहने वाली अप्सराएँ भी दुर्लभ नहीं।)

कामधातु समतिक्कमा गति, रूपधातुया भावो न दुल्लभो।
वीतरागविसयूपपत्ति या, ये चरन्ति पमदाहनत्थिका।।
(जो ख्रियों के प्रति अनासक्त रहते हैं उन्हें काम धातु के अतिक्रमण से प्राप्त होने वाली गति तथा रूप धातु

का भाव भी दुर्लभ नहीं, और वीतरागों का उत्पत्ति स्थान शुद्धवास लोक भी दुर्लभ नहीं।)

सब्बदुक्खसमत्तिक्कमम् सिवम्, अच्चन्तमचलितम् असङ्खतम्।
निब्बुतेहि सुचिही न दुल्लभम्, ये चरन्ति पमदाहनत्थिका' ति।।
(जो स्त्रियों के प्रति अनासक्त रहते हैं उन पवित्र विरक्तों को सब दुःखों का अंत-स्वरूप, शिव-स्वरूप, अविनाश-स्वरूप, स्थिर-स्वरूप, असंस्कृत-निर्वाण भी दुर्लभ नहीं।)

'Videh' Arvind Kumar
Aashrum, Lucknow, UP, India
August, 2024

Transcripts of *Hindee* letters and *maatraas*

Keeping in view the special pronunciations of *Sanskrit* words, and with a view to differentiating between the disparate pronunciations, we have followed the following regimen of transcription from *Devnaagaree* to Roman script. This clarification will help the readers appreciate the nuances of linguistic specificities and enjoy the text in truly desired sense. Moreover, the vernacular words, particularly nouns, have been italicized.

अ a, आ aa, इ i, ई ee, उ u, ऊ oo, ऋ ri, ए e, ऐ ai, ओ o, औ ऑ au, अं an, अ: :,
क ka, का kaa, कि ki, की kee, कु ku, कू koo, कृ kri, के ke, कै kai, को ko, कौ kau, कं kan, क: kah;

1. Cycle Turns Full Circle
Enter Protagonist

I had completed my session at the school and at the fag-end thereof I had worked as the wood-cutter for my mother, with a view to fetching stock of fire-wood for her despite being a gifted child -- and this was being executed even when the academic session was on, that is, the final exams were going on. However, the existential problems had precedence over academic and romantic issues of life. Session ended, annual summer vacations were declared, and we made it to our maternal relatives' house, our *Nanihaal,* without losing a day's time. That was a given. And we kids were very glad to go to that Elysium of our childhood. Sometimes I used to muse that we went there as a right, as though it were our second home, and without feeling any inhibition in our heart, and without any rancour – at least overt – on the part of our benefactors, whereas we had never seen the children of our maternal uncles going to their maternal uncles and aunts, in turn. And that paradox puzzled me a lot. In fact the kids of our maternal fraternity were fortunate ones, whilst we were wretches, kids of shameless fellows, worthless issues of an all the more good-for-nothing lad called our father. It was only later that I realized that ours was a special case, a case of wretched living, worthless existence, and at the same time one of conceit, of showing off as a worthy pedigree, instead.

And as the time never stops – however long a time-limit might be set, it ultimately comes to an end – the one month or so long a period of our summer vacations, too, came to an end. It was 1969 summer season. I had no clue as to the precarious condition my mother was in as regards her stay at her in-laws – our paternal village -- in the absence of her husband. Moreover, her husband, despite being employed as an *ad hoc* teacher at a far off village, was of no use for the household of mother at our village; rather, he used to snatch away whatever small money my mother possessed. To meet the expenses of her household and those of my schooling she depended frequently on the kindly relatives there.

In the month of July when the schools did open and when I was craving for going back to my school back at *Inaayatpur,* I noticed that there was no move at all towards that end at our maternal relatives' household. My mother was showing no signs of going back to the village, even as, she was making no preparations. Nor did anybody come from our father's side to take us back to the village. I at times wondered how my father did live all alone at his village during the summer vacations and how did he manage to cook his food etc. there.

He had little sense of duty towards his small family's upkeep and maintenance, nor did he possess an iota of shame regarding having onloaded his share of burden on his in-laws. The ever upset mood of my elder maternal uncle and at times of my maternal grandfather and their ruthful behaviour towards me and my mother, and their subjecting us to all sorts of harsh physical labour as well as menial chores including errands to be attended in the agricultural fields was indicative enough of their dislike for our arrival at theirs. Yet we were least wary of it all, nor was my mother, however, subconsciously she might have been; I was not as a child of almost twelve.

When nobody turned up, nor did come any postcard from our father even by the second week of July, 1969, it was decided as a distress decision to send me to *Jaabil* school as an *ad hoc* student along with other kids of the household. They might be morose and sad, my mother might be feeling depressed by this unwarranted development, yet I as a child was happy. I was getting to stay back at my *Nanihaal* that was nothing short of an Elysium for me, and also, I was going to get the company of my two cousin maternal sisters while going to school! I was a brilliant child no doubt at the new school as well, and the teachers there came to realise that soon.

This *Jaabil* school was at an open space, in an erstwhile fertile agricultural field, amidst the greenery and rich vegetation. It was well kept, as well, and was full of vegetation and mesmerizing flower-beds were abounding in it. The teachers there were almost all under the awe of our maternal relatives' aura and status, and almost all of them were related closely or distantly with our family. That was another factor why I was getting a respectful and caressing treatment from the teachers there.

Under all these circumstances I was happy at least to think that we did not have to live in the company of such a vile creature as our father was; he was a constant source of stress and distress for other creatures in the household except for himself. He had been a druggist in the past I think and a boozer, now I come to realise in hindsight. And a madman, in literal sense, as was vouchsafed by many people later on.

It was exactly there at *Jaabil* school that during one morning assembly, in a very ebullient mood, our Principal – *Pancham Singh* – and other smart and dynamic teachers declared that 'It is a great day in the history of mankind that MAN HAS REACHED THE MOON!' The youthful teacher had declared in a loud voice as though the entire population of earth had been transmigrated to the surface of moon. It was actually the ascent of Neil

Armstrong onto the moon, his setting foot on the surface of the Moon. That was really a great news! Throughout the day, there was an atmosphere of joy and merriment. It was a moment of victory for the humanity as a whole! Collectively!

However, resourceful the humanity might be, even to reach the moon, or even the seventh sky, I mused, my lot and that of my indolent and inert father was not going to improve an inch. I was not getting to live at my own village or at my own disposal. We had to live at the mercy of others forever! The humanity's victory over nature did not arouse any sense of pride in my heart, I tell you.

My father had gone back to his school at *Veerpuraa*. Our shelter home at our village was locked and latched. I was little concerned; that was not my bidding.

Having been married prematurely, or forcibly, so to say, in 1952, it was now almost 17 years, yet that lad of 35 had not been able to set his two feet on the ground. He was ever playing a victim card, feeling no qualms of conscience as regards his duty towards those begotten by him through sexual intercourse with his wife.

My study was going on well under the temporary arrangement, and two or three months had elapsed when one day, instead of receiving any good news from our father, my mother received a heartening news that my father was seriously sick.

"Your father is very seriously sick!", my mother informed me with a face downcast.

"How sick? What sickness?", I asked innocently.

"Very sick! He has sickness connected with the urinating organ!", conveyed my mother sensibly hiding the obscenity associated with the organ of sickness.

I could not fathom anything. How could I? Although I had myself as a child been abused the year gone by! I tried to associate my father's sexual disease to something like that.

That was a good *alibi* for our maternal relatives to get rid of us, and for my mother an obligation to pack there and go to her husband's village. Without any ado, we hurried back to our village; I expecting my father about to die or having already died, for I had the impression that even if someone might have died the sad news would never be conveyed as such to one's relatives, especially, those coming from far off places. And to my surprise, my mother got perturbed at her husband's disease and imminent death! I was wondering why she should be sad at the death of such a devilish husband who was so cruel and of no use for her. However, he was! He had already impregnated her during the last winter with my younger brother *Raakesh* in her womb. Carnal desires is what mattered to her and why my father was needed as a living entity.

Father had come back from *Veerpuraa* and was in the village. Fortunately for us, he did not seem to be as sick as was made out to be through the missive and the messenger. His penis had been infected by some disease that obstructed his urinating, and it caused unbearable pain while urinating. We soon realized within a day or two that he was in utter pain.

When they thought that I and my sister were asleep – though we were not - they chatted amongst themselves intimately, sharing their woes and soft sides. I then realized that however cruel a husband might show before the outer society and others during the day, one does show only the soft side to one's woman at night. That was an other worldly experience for me! I nonetheless drew some solace from this revelation! Nonetheless, that was no consolation during the daytime; father was as devilish during the day as he ever was. And he remained as such throughout his very long life. Here I recall Hermann Hesse who proclaimed through one of his characters that out of delusion the creatures take the outworldly things and creatures including human beings as real whilst in actuality the only reality that there is dwells within oneself, not outside.

Daily we saw many people and many doctors, *vaidyas* and *hakeems* visiting my father prescribing different types of remedies, potions, concoctions, drugs, herbs and medicines etc. Because there was extreme burning sensation in the penis, most of the sensible persons suggested cold butter-milk to be consumed as a drink as a remedy or medicine. However, there was no dearth of butter-milk in the broader family fold, although there was no wherewithal to have butter-milk in our own, our father's family. After vacillating between aggravation and mollification the disease finally subsided to some extent. After, of course, a few months!

In the meantime, I had started going to the *Inaayatpur* school. Somewhat feeling like a luckless and lacklustre person who despite being a prodigy had no wherewithal for schooling. At my old school – *Inaayatpur* – the school authorities had been enquiring of my elder uncle – who was also a teacher there – why I had not come back to attend the school, and my uncle had disclosed that it was due to lack of wherewithal that I was constrained to stay away from schooling. To which, my kindly school manager – *Raajpaal Singh* – who was otherwise seemingly so tough by countenance, is reported to have offered that he would allow me fees concession, I being a prodigy of their school.

When I came back, it was not because I had been given concession in fees, but because my fate brought me back there in the shape of my father's supposedly fatal sexual disease. And my classmates, especially, my lovers – the beautiful lasses – became so happy! And they expressed it evocatively, by their effusive faces in welcoming me. Even my friend, the son of our Principal, heaved a sigh of relief that I had come back at the last.

However, on my mind, I had my father as a sick person. My father had given up *ad hoc* job, too however, in the process, or as a fallout.

XXX

Table of Contents

2.*Father's Sins and Libel*

Enter Protagonist

For months together, father continued to be bed-ridden; nay, he could walk, he could go to the nature's call of his own; and that was a great consolation for us to believe that he was not going to die, at least soon. However, I kept on wondering why the missive that was given us when we were at our maternal relative's home was so precarious. Maybe that was used as an *alibi* so as to send us packing to our father's land. It was too much for my maternal relatives now to keep the married girl at their home for so long; already she had been there one year back lock, stock and barrel.

A fanciful thought crossed my skull those days. For father's demeanour was devilish, and for he was not an affable and loveable personage, I fancied if my father died how happy and stress-free we would all be! But that was not to be. We were destined to bear the brunt of his deranged skull for decades, nay, for half a century thereafter.

During those days of perfect unemployment and total dearth of any earning who was bearing the costs of living of us all I sometimes wonder now; albeit at that juncture, I had little concern for all those matters. This anxiety didn't even cross my mind. My mother would be bearing the brunt all through, I suppose. Moreover, her parental establishment was very caring, and they might be helping her financially, I am sure.

We were brought back from our *Nanihaal* again by the same person, our omnipresent uncle – *Modhoo chaachaajee* – this time as well. Last year too, this was he only who had brought us back here after my fifth standard schooling. Not only he had brought us back, his younger sister did sleep with our family for the entire year as an added safeguard for my young mother against the evil-doers of vulgar society. And evil-doers there were, no doubt. My mother was young and pretty; and I despite being a teenager could spot certain scoundrels making rounds of the big compound – the cattle pasture

– in front of our refugee house, eyeing my mother passing thereby for instance, for nature's call or the like activities.

Even the *Desho buaa* who was acting as our safeguard during night time was young only at that time; and that was another, doubly risky proposition. As regards that prospect, as the son of our barber used to visit us daily in the evening, i.e.; before bed-time, we took it as an innocuous gesture on the part of an innocent youth; however, not all the villagers harboured the same notions; they apprehended something fishy on the youth's part as regards his intentions in visiting our homestead. They resented as to why a young boy should visit our family daily in the evening, whereas we as children felt our morale boosted with his presence. After some time *Omee* stopped visiting us, to our disappointment. *Omee* was his name in colloquial parlance. Prior to his stopping visiting our home we had noticed that his father used to hail him from outside: *'Omee! Omee! Come here, what are you doing there?' et al.* Now when he stopped seeing us, we realised the physical significance and implied meaning of those distressed calls by our barber, his aged father. We missed our evening children's tales that *Omee* used to tell us daily as well as interestingly. Not only that, he was acting as a news correspondent for

us, too; and that was very interesting as well as intriguing for us kids. That way we were gaining currency in the society without exerting at all on our part.

When we enquired of our mother why *Omee Bhaiyaa* had stopped visiting us, my mother simply announced that his parents forbade him from doing so; also that the villagers including the family members of *Desho buaajee* had raised objections to *Omee* visiting us in this way, especially, at night. We wondered as kids why anybody should have objections to *Omee Bhaiyaa's* altruistic visits to our shelter home. He was sort of our honorary caretaker, particularly, psychic.

Thus our father was out of job in an absolute sense. Perfectly without any means! Later on, we realised that he had usurped one hundred rupees from the Principal of his school prior to falling sick, sort of embezzlement of the funds of the school fees collected by him. For the period of his sickness, this did not come to the notice of anybody, but when he recovered, almost after six months, the lender – the Principal – started visiting my father frequently for recovery of his debt, for he was having his in-laws in our village only.

In this context, I could recollect the tale narrated by my father during the weeding of millet field years later. My father had told that the school had not paid his wages for months together; such was the condition of most of the educational institutions those days. The managements had opened those schools simply for their own selfish motives: to earn money. They did not pay any regular pay-outs to the teachers who were mostly appointed as *ad hoc* servants ever at the disposal and mercy of the management. In such dire straits how the poor teachers managed their home affairs is anybody's guesswork. They relied on tuitions and on prescribing unnecessary books in the classes for a commission from the book-sellers. Such vile activities, that did not behove of the community of teachers! But what could those poor people do, their designation being teachers or preceptors notwithstanding? Some of them were nothing short of scoundrels as well, to be frank.

My father was not getting his wages. He mentioned this problem to one of his colleagues, and the wily guy – as he himself would have been – suggested to my skull-less father that the latter should keep the fees collected from the class unto himself and not deposit the same in the office with the cashier. A person lacking common sense as he was, my father followed the guidance literally and embezzled two hundred rupees. And those two hundred rupees became the bone in the flesh of my father's throat *(galey kee haddee)* for decades thereafter. He decided not to pay back those two hundred rupees to the kindly lenders and made them to visit him almost figuratively hundred times. Both the husband and wife came umpteen number of times to recover their petty sum and at times even created ugly scenes throughout the village, but to no effect on the morale or countenance of my shameless father.

When I asked my father why he did not pay off the embezzled sum at the earliest, his reply was, "I had decided to teach them a lesson!"

But he never disclosed why? Why he wanted to teach them a lesson? That was his typical nature; he used to act irrationally and illogically, as a deranged species does normally. He was acting against his benefactor who had helped him salvage his prestige in the wake of embezzlement, even though out of compulsion.

Maybe that was the same seed of sin whereby my father's penis got inflicted with the sexual disease!

However, for lasting treatment of the dreaded disease, my elder uncle and aunt took my father to their place, *Ajmer,* where my uncle was employed in Railways, and where they had a doctor of their acquaintance, also, of our caste, and one who was even distantly related to them. In the hope that it would be a cheaper option. My father went there for he had no other option left, moneyless as he was. Here, at the village, we were again *sans* any male support, my mother bearing the whole burden of the household. However, the relatives and kindly villagers might be helping her in her days of penury.

But one thing was for sure: that we kids were feeling relieved with the father not being around, for his presence around was a sure shot source of stress and arguments and ill-will. Those few months of our life were lived in perfect serenity and peace of mind.

Father had never been at good or talking terms with my uncle and aunt with whom he was obliged to go to their place for treatment. But in such straitjacket circumstances he had no other option. After a few months he did return, cured to some extent, but full of ill-will and bad opinion about the doctor who was supposed to have treated him there, that is, the acquaintance of our uncle. The reason for my father's disenchantment with the doctor, instead of being grateful to him, was disclosed to me somewhat later when during the following summer our uncle visited the village for disposing and settling of the agricultural produce and matters. I was accompanying them – him and his elder son, the paedophile – to the town. Yet another villager – our

uncle of close relationship – was also accompanying us to see them off. Out of compassion towards us kids of our wretched father, the uncle in question requested to our outgoing uncle that they should make some arrangement for my father's employment at *Ajmer* itself so that we could survive. The uncle even suggested that they might explore the possibility of arranging some tuitions for my father for he was supposed to be good at English teaching.

The son of my uncle at this benevolent suggestion retorted back contemptuously, "Fuck his English teaching! He knows nothing in English; he has simply conned certain sentences and keeps on teaching only those to the foolish pupils!"

At this unexpected as well as outrageous allegation of the lad against my father, not only my uncle, but also, I felt deeply hurt. The guy was a scoundrel, a paedophile, a seducer, a rapist, I knew it well – having been myself a sufferer of his own depravity. How could he dare accuse my father of such a wily thing. My father had a high reputation as an English teacher in the rural hinterland around my village. In a single unconcerned stroke the scoundrel had shattered my father's prestige in this way. My zeal for taking their baggage to the town got diminished. My elder uncle did however not utter a word; he simply chuckled, indicating that what his son had remarked had some truth in it. And I also started feeling that my father's teaching style was in fact like that only. He could teach only grammar and translation, but his pupils could not speak English, for speaking a language takes movement of tongue, too, not only writing on parchments.

The guy did not stop only there; when our villager uncle enquired what the disease of my father was as diagnosed by the domestic doctor, he disclosed peevishly that the doctor had disclosed that such disease was contracted by indulging in illegitimate sexual activities like having sex with prostitutes etc. That was shocking for us all. However, nobody spoke anything; they had given long rope to the youth, he himself being a sexual abuser notwithstanding. All this conversation that day was too much for me; I lost all regard for both the son and the father. I realised that they were not our benefactors; they were rather cheats and selfish scoundrels, seeking excuses for getting rid of the eventuality of helping us. The lad also disclosed that some tuitions were arranged for my father at *Ajmer*, but the latter could not take them.

Oh, how sham was my father's skill even of English language! He had already squandered his period of education and training, squandering side by side the jewellery of his wife and even the emotive bangles of his small kid, and now he was possessing no skills whereby he could survive the life, what to speak of meeting the necessaries of life for his family! There was gloom before my eyes, before my future!

At home, however, I had heard my father narrating umpteen number of times the cause of his sexual disease as the usage of *Sulphaas*. Here, let me clarify that my father was very fond of consuming drugs and medicines; even without any cause he would like to have allopathic and all sorts of drugs. He seemed to be a drug addict. Indeed he had been a drug addict while staying with his relatives during his failed B.Ed. training at *Ganj Dundwaaraa*. Now when he had come away from his wily relatives, he had been addicted to medicines and all sorts of tablets, herbs etc. And for that excess he suffered. He told my mother that for a small disease he had consulted a quack who as usual claimed himself to be a great curer and he suggested *Sulphaas* as medicine for the disease and the result was the inflammatory disease of the urinary organ and system, leading my father to the door of death.

I never could bring myself to believe that my father would have indulged in any illegitimate sexual intercourse with any lady, what to speak of prostitutes. He was certainly not made of that stuff, however indolent and mindless he was.

XXX

Table of Contents

3. Peasants Don't Know How To Plough The Fields

Enter Protagonist

In the standard seventh when I resumed my classes after having been forced by circumstances to come back to our village in the wake of my father's unmentionable disease, I was an established prodigy at school, an unchallenged one. And the teachers without exception adored me; not because I was the son of my father, who was a teacher himself at yet another school in the geographical area, but because I really was an innately gifted chap. Moreover, I was handsome, the proof of which was that all the girls without exception felt attracted towards me; I am sanguine that attraction was not purely on account of my giftedness and academic brilliance, but also, because I was a handsome and glamorous lad.

However, brilliant I might have been in academic terms, that was no guarantee that I would be expert in all the spheres of life, society or world at large.

In the town there at another place, there was one teacher, *K Raaj Singh,* who was one of the fast friends of my father. He often used to visit our village, I had observed, and he used to chat with my grandfather voraciously, for my grandfather was a sort of reservoir of academic knowledge, at least in that illiterate milieu. One of the younger brothers of this *K Raaj Singh* was teacher in our village school, and he taught us history, apart from teaching *Hindee.* That he taught us history I can vouch from the fact that I can still recollect his lessons given us concerning the civilization of *Mohan-jo-Daro* and the valley of *Sindhu* river. I was highly impressed by those lessons, not because he was any extraordinary orator or teacher, but because the revelation of this fact aroused in my mind the fancy that the extinguished civilization would have been nothing but the *Vaidic* civilization only. And for the settlements fell on the path of invaders coming from the *Arabian* and the farther countries, those human habitations were plundered and annihilated without a trace; and in the course of time had been subsumed by the sand and dust of mother earth as usual. Everything on the surface of earth keeps on getting drowned and drowned into its depths. I might be harbouring this notion, however, my semi-literate teacher was not: he kept on harping on the same theme as was written in the book held in his hand: it was an unknown civilization. What unknown! It is obvious, it was *Vaidic* civilization, destroyed in the medieval era by marauders of western lands.

Yet another encounter with this not-so-knowledgeable teacher was regarding an essay that he asked us pupil to write in the *Hindee* period on Agriculture in India. I wrote the essay using best possible words and flowery sentences, however, without substance and *sans* the actual facts, and thought that it was me that would be declared as the best essay-writer on the basis of the notion that I was on top in respect of all other subjects and matters. Moreover, for I was the crown of the class and the lasses!

When my piece of parchment containing the essay reached the hands of my teacher, I observed, instead of getting amused or instead of appreciating my essay, he laughed boisterously before the class which was not his wont usually; he was a hard-faced, emotionless *Jaat* youth. A peasant himself by birth. I was dumbfounded. I was sure I would have written nothing wrong as regards spellings. Then why was the teacher derisive of my performance, surprisingly for me.

And soon he started reeling off the *faux pas* I had made. He started reading my essay aloud before the class. He emphasised the sentences like this : 'the farmers in India do not know how to plough the fields, that is why the condition of agriculture in India is bad and the farmers are poor....', and no sooner had he uttered these words than the whole class burst into loud laughter and uproar. My teacher added in mock derision, *'Eh,* if your father does not know how to plough the fields, it does not mean that no farmer in India knows how to plough the fields. Farmers in India pretty well know how and when to plough their fields!'

I felt ashamed and humiliated before the class. But my narration of facts was correct. I was correct so far as my knowledge went; my father did not know how to plough the fields with the help of bullocks and plough. But my kindly teacher had himself clarified the situation that my elitist father, being from a feudal society and pedigreed family, might not be knowing how to plough, but that did not go to prove that no farmer in India knew how to plough the fields.

This *faux pas* on my part reached the ears of my father at the town school through the friend of my father, for the episode was so hilarious that our teacher might have conveyed the same to his elder brother – *K Raaj Singh* – and he, in turn, enjoyed repeating the episode in his school before my father and other teachers. I came to know of it when my father repeated the mirthful episode before me in the evening. But instead of feeling ashamed, he felt proud of his lack of skill as regards ploughing, for with a view to be fit into the standards of feudalism it was essential that one should have been indolent and ignorant in all the skills that help earn a living.

However, I developed a sense of deprivation and loss as I felt that given my parent's exceptional qualities that did not fit into the rut of society I might be losing sight of many a reality, and in turn, I might be hoodwinked into believing certain illusions and half-truths as ultimate truths.

XXX

Table of Contents

4. Onslaught Of Nymphs

Enter protagonist

Oh, lo, I set off bombarding you with my 'philosophy'! That's the gravest weakness of any intellectual, a sham one, like me! Every intellectual, say author, deigns oneself to be a philosopher. I was taking you along to introduce you to *Raajeshwaree!* Haven't I? You might be focussed thither yet I too am habitual to flaunting my anecdotes, incidents or things of lesser interest onto you. You may guard your interests whilst I am doing mine. In this melodrama of self-aggrandisement! Yet, pray, keep in tandem with me.

Autumn! It's too cold inside the class-room, too cold. The class-room is un-plastered, merely walled by brickwork. Rustic environs these are! They have to be like that only. No surprise! Our Extension Teacher – the teacher of Agriculture in simple parlance - is teaching us. Wow! Splendid! What a grand, stout and impressive, personality is this of the Extension Teacher! Very frightening too! Terrorising to students! Nobody could dare him? Students could have pleaded with any other *aacharya*, but who could muster courage to plead with *Jaageshwar Prasaad Sharmaa* for taking the students out in the sunshine and teach there in the warmth of the sun? Everyone is constrained to continue with study even while shivering with cold – in this chilled wintery weather.

"*Paapaa*, why don't you take us in the sun? It's too cold inside here!"

Eh, Paapaa? Who's *Paapaa?* This is *Raajeshwaree,* the same flowery girl, a budding beauty, fragrant alike a blossom, standing in the class and entreating, pointing to the Extension-Teacher. I shuddered as soon as I learned that the Extension Teacher was her father. I marvelled also at the confounding contrast of the two: the father and the daughter, to contemplate that the originating source, the cave, from which this soft bud, this tender soul, *Raajeshwaree*, had emanated was such a cruel, hard-hearted persona as our Extension Teacher, *Jaageshwar Prasaad Sharmaa.* I could not believe it for a while; it took some time for this bizarre reality to sink in. I asked my classmate sitting beside, "*Hoshiyaar Singh,* why is she calling this stone-hearted teacher as her *Paapaa?*"

"If she has him as father, she is addressing him as such!" rejoindered my friend, somewhat bemused. However, I felt amazed.

"Well! Is it?"

The mind began to dive – dive into the ocean of unknown feelings galore. As if trying to resolve the mystery that such a soft bodied, so soft, so tender, so sweet, so attractive, so enamouring a girl, one having such a sweet heart, with so beautiful and slender lips, endowed with a tone that poured nectar when she spoke, how could she be the daughter of such a hard-hearted man, whom even the teachers, his colleagues, dreaded, what to speak of poor students!

And more than that, I am witness to a spectacle which gives rise to a bigger amazement on my countenance in that the same Extension Teacher is spreading a smile on his otherwise stern face. This smile is unprecedented and unforeseen heretofore, a smile that reminds me of the amplified phase of the most enrapturing smile ever present on the beauteous countenance of *Raajeshwaree*. The bewilderment clouding the mind thus far disappeared in a moment. Her father also possessed the same bewitching smile, and also, the same sweet, sonorous voice, "Well, children! Let's move to the sunshine outside; it's very cold inside here today."

The children were very happy. They looked towards the victorious girl with a sense of gratitude. There was no question of giving thanks or expressing gratitude towards her, for no such decency or mores had been imparted to them by anybody, neither through tradition nor through sacrament. Theirs was a life being lived in an immature or amateur way. It was not a well-groomed life. They let their tender feelings be felt towards that lovely piece of life die within their hearts. It was not in vogue to converse with girls freely and frankly; that was sort of a taboo. Yet, she herself did not let it go past her. She seemed to be basking in the glory of her accomplishment, the accomplishment of prodding her father to come out in the sun. The pride of getting her notoriously 'tough father' to agree to her request! The opportunity to flaunt to her friends and other students her influence!

"Just saw it! My father loves me very much. He cannot refuse my entreaties." She was telling *Roopwatee, alias Munnee.*

Even after moving into sunshine, the children were in no mood to continue with the studies, nor was the teacher in a mood to teach. He let everybody loose and then ventured to suggest of his own, "Well, come on, let me tell you all an interesting story."

"Yes, yes, *Maassaab!*", the children cackled even as their countenances blossomed.

"Someone of you, do fetch me your English Reader; let's read from it."

He set off teaching the familiar story of two cats and a monkey. After a while he paused and said, *"Raajesh! Raajeshwaree!"* The girl became wary. She was probably gossiping with her friend, *Munnee.*

Then once again, the teacher paused and shouted sternly, *"Raajeshwaree!* Now it will be very bad if there is any more mischief and gossip!"

But the mischief continued and it was for the third time, and *Pandit Jaageshwar Prasaad Sharmaa* made me stand up instead of the girl. I was shaken to the bone. He beckoned me. Somehow I approached him, trembling in my under wears. I didn't know which crime had inadvertently happened on my part?

"Arvind! You are very smart. You don't need to listen to this story. You do one thing..."

Immediately I was rid completely of all the doubts and misgivings.

"Jee, Maassaab?"

"You take this girl away!........"

Now I was not at all prepared for this eventuality. That was an anathema for me! To talk to a girl and least of all, to sit beside her, in close-up, in close proximity!

The words had not even emerged completely from his lips that my heart came to a standstill. Stop it did to a throb! The excitement, the zeal that had emerged on my countenance a short while ago diminished and went into oblivion. An unexpected incident, unwarranted occurrence had taken place. Unimaginable! Such an adorable, such an enchanting damsel, was being given to me by her harsh and stern father of his own free will and volition.

Nonetheless, I was not enthused; rather, I was drowning in the ocean of melancholy, of depression. Reason was the thought, the apprehension, that after this incident, after this rendezvous with a damsel of a girl, how would I be eligible for having salvaged my vow of celibacy – the *Brahmacharya!* Girls should be avoided! They should not even be peeked at! One should not talk to them at all! Don't even muse or think about them in your mind! Lest the vow of celibacy – the *Brahmacharya* - should be shattered! Thereafter, no hope of, no prospects for, securing good marks in the exams! And exams for me were the be all and end all. As if I and all others were studying and attending schools only for securing high marks! As though securing highest marks in the exams was the only aim, as also, means of life! This was my line of thinking as regards the almost half the population of the planet! And exactly this was the input given me by my saviours and by those who had brought me up!

This was my philosophy for conversing with anybody, or the mores for an ideal child, which were imbibed in my psyche by my environs and social surroundings!

It seems like going to the farthest end of the pendulum of restraints.

It used to be preached to me at home off and on:

Maatraa swastraa duhitraa vaa,
Na cha viviktaasano bhavet,
Balvaanamindriya graamo,
Vidwaansamapi karshati!

(मात्रा स्वस्त्रा दुहित्रा वा
न च विविक्तासनो भवेत
बलवानमिंद्रिय ग्रामो
विद्वांसमपि कर्षति!)

(Meaning thereby, one should not sit in isolation or solitude on the same seat or bed along with even one's mother, wife, or daughter, for these strong carnal senses can vanquish even the greatest scholars!)

This was the height; height of hypocrisy! Climactic instructions! With proportions of extremity!

If a tendency has such a strong propensity, such an intensive impact on psyche, definitely it cannot be an unnatural and sham tendency. A wrong, amorous, immoral, artificial or unnatural tendency can never be so strong and intensive. If

that's considered so, certainly there is something drastically wrong with the thinking and perceptions of the human beings, the society, as regards the life's philosophy. The man had better scrap such norms shunning conceit, forsaking prejudice *et al.*

Nonetheless, I observed that this lesson of maintaining an attitude of alienation, aloofness, rather untouchability, towards the women folks was being taught a little too much fervently in our family to the upcoming generations. Especially, to the generations begotten post that gory episode! The episode of *Pradhaan Baabaa* and *Mukundee, Veerendra's* mother. That was also the valid reason - the compelling cause, virtually. The nose of the area's largest family had been chopped off a few years back − exactly for this lecherousness towards a woman. The story goes somewhat as follows.

XXX

Table of Contents

5. *Hell-fire Of Carnal Passions*
Enter protagonist

Drigpaal Pradhaan found it as a very good opportunity, an opportune time! It was winter season. Extremely chilled cold. On top of that, *Raamleelaa* was being played in the village. Every village folk must be assembled there. No one would come to know of it. The slimy job! The misadventure of making love, having sex with a widowed young lady!

And the young and youthful *Pradhaan* – the administrative head of the village – dashed into *Mukundee's* house. Her paramour! Widowed just a few months back! Every limb of her seductive youthful body was palpitating with carnal desire – the nature's sweetest blessing, the sweetest curse of Adam and Eve bestowed upon them in the garden of Eden! Her breasts had been as though thrusting forth trying to come out of the clothing whatever she was wearing! The arms and armpits were longing intensively for getting masqueraded or massaged in a pains-giving manner! The whole body looked like a smouldering fire! Fire, which does not have any conscience, does not bother any social norms! Fire, which, when it arises, incinerates everything, be it the books of morals, or the wooden boxes, or even a thatched straw roof! The fire that burns even the clothes for the person and strips him or her to the bones! To be left entirely naked and nude!

So, to avoid the fire, *Mukundee* within no time stripped herself totally, took off all her clothes, and threw them aside. Clothes scattered all around on the floor! Telling the pathetic tale of a young woman's hurt aspirations and shattered dreams who had only recently been married and her husband had died untimely! But this fire is not extinguished by taking off the clothes, or by stripping oneself totally, it rather flares up even more powerfully. It overwhelms every other passion and thought at that time. Fire! It got subsumed through the strong young arms of the *Pradhaan* into her heart and thighs and in the arena where it derives ultimate solace and satisfaction.

It would have continued for time immemorial had not the firefighters of society arrived on the scene in time! The fire had just then completely devoured its fuel; there was no other performance left to be done anymore! The fire would have subsided and finally extinguished of its own, as well, as every flare up ultimately subsides and dies, but the rage of the society set off raining heavily through the strokes of sticks and spears. On the body and back of *Pradhaan!* With *Mukundee* trying frenetically to intervene so as to protect her seducer and justify the episode but to no avail! *Mukundee's* family members had already broken into the house by smashing the doors and jumping inside. Sticks and spears! All jingling and jangling! And left there was but the smashed and thrashed body of *Pradhaan*: all bone-marrowy, all broken-boned! The wretch had almost died.

Once declared 'amorous', 'immoral' or for a thousand times called 'immoral' or 'amorous', it makes little difference. Seeing her paramour, giver of the highest degree of carnal pleasure to her passionately charged body, in this moribund state immediately after the sexual act, *Mukundee* forgot the pain and memory of even her widowhood. She threw away the sham veil of social shame thrust upon women folks by male society. Within an instant, she metamorphosed into an unabashed and bold lady whom some even dubbed as shameless.

To guard against the vagaries of weathers and seasons she put on the clothes to cover her body, but she did nothing to cover her shame: she forsook forever the veil, the cloth covering her face. The same shy young lass who had come to this village as a lovely and seductive bride only a few years back had turned into a rebel, an unabashed lady, a sort of vampire!

This *Drigpaal Pradhaan* was part of my own affluent family. That is, with the happening of this slimy episode the nose of the father's family was cut off forever like the nose of mythological *Soorpanakhaa*. At least that's what my family's impression was. Anyway, the fear of the people that lingered in their minds about this family ended decisively. The awe the family cast over the lesser mortals of the area had gone. They became bold. They refused to suffer any further injustice or inequity. They were as though waiting for this opportunity! They were as though observing the episode unfold, rather, escalate further, to the point where they could inflict incurable hurt on the prestige of the feudal fiefdom of our family.

My family used to do injustice before – big injustices, but the people and society which were forced to obey earlier without a word of grudge, had now become assertive and courageous. The 'immorality', the 'amorous act' of a single individual had shorn the entire prestigious family of the privileged position as regards reverence and submissiveness from the common folks. The veil from amorous activities of the members of the feudal family had been blown off! Prior to that, too, all that was going on, but then everything kept happening under the veil, the veil of secrecy, under awe and fear of the strongmen of the family.

Was the young chieftain the first lecherous and lustful impatient luxuriant depraved chap? No, he was the last one when viewed in absolute terms! And probably he got such a harsh punishment of making love in the first instance itself. Such a novice! Nevertheless, the erstwhile youth of the family had not left untouched any of the so-called 'untouchable' daughters and daughters-in-law. But who could ever find them doing any such unseemly thing in the glare of daylight when they would be looking towards a girl or a wife of anybody, whose house they used to frequent so nonchalantly at night and indulge in all sorts of amorous activities.

There were many a man of *'shoodra'* clan whose mothers had told them the names of their real fathers as being from amongst the people of my elite family; and the latter were seen, too, giving their illegitimate issues the love and affection of real fathers. And it all was an open secret! Still treated as a top secret! That was typical of the feudal norms and morality! Such men – illegitimate ones - and their families were comparatively wealthier than the families of those whose daughters and daughters-in-law had refused to give in to the amorous advances of the members of my family, if only at the risk of reprisals and dread. Morality has always been instrumental in making the humanity starve! Ironically, money has ever been a panacea for immorality! Rather immorality has been a panacea for earning wealth!

Nonetheless, there is a bug created deliberately in the software program of the human society whereby it is ensured that whoever does not fall in line, does not obey the commands, one should be forced into submission, creating existential problems, creating shortages of necessaries of life, cutting the supply line of essential ingredients of life for such recalcitrant folks. Don't let them dwell anywhere, don't let them afford two morsels of food, put their straw huts to fire, rage their habitats, don't let them collect even dry twigs of trees to be used as fuel for making fire, don't let their children go to school and study, torture and terrorise even their issues and progeny in the same manner as their elders and predecessors were tortured and terrorised!

Is it a lone story?

Therefore, there was a palpable sense of toeing the line of the ancestors. They got impatient and started feeling insecure with the happening of this episode. The erstwhile generations, prior to that, were possibly not taught or preached the lessons of celibacy – the *Brahmacharya*. That is why it was my generation that had just descended on the scene of the family canvas, in the glare of the Creation, still somewhat somnolent and still blinking the eyes, which was being made very vigorously to be entirely averse to the fair sex, or to have anything to do with the fair sex. The gynophobia!

It seems as if this feudal family fiefdom had no prior experience of deciding as to how much this species of the Creation – forming half the population of the universe – should be mingled with, and how much should it be maintained distance from. Therefore, it was I who had to bear the brunt of this, and I was repeatedly preached:

Maatraa swastraa duhitraa vaa

Na cha viviktaasano bhavet
Balvaanamindriya graamo
Vidwaansamapi karshati!
(मात्रा स्वस्रा दुहित्रा वा
न च विविक्तासनो भवेत
बलवानमिंद्रिय ग्रामो
विद्वांसमपि कर्षति!)

(Meaning thereby, one should not sit in isolation or solitude on the same seat or bed along with even one's mother, wife, or daughter, for these strong carnal senses can vanquish even the greatest scholars!)

Yes, that is why I say: these are the heights of hypocrisy, the crazy instructions, of imposed injunctions. Travesty of what is called morality! There was no limit left for mores and morality! Just 'Nip in the Bud' seemed to be the distressed knee jerk reaction of that gory episode.

Will ever a person who is descending on the stage of life and world be able to develop oneself into a full-fledged human being within this straitjacket trap of morality without any leeway at all? He would be paralyzed – paralyzed he would be psychologically! As I have become! An awkward personality, a *bodom* male species of homo sapiens!

XXX

Table of Contents

6. *Love's Labour Lost*

Enter protagonist

Raajeshwaree was sitting very tight and as *chhuyee-muyee* (a shame plant), she was sort of shorn of speech. All her naughtiness, her fidgetiness, her ever readiness to nag me, trouble me, *et al* all was absent, all that had as if deserted her! How that happened I wondered? I drew some solace from the fact that it was not only me that was abashed in company of an opposite sex, but also, she was equally abashed and shy. Now when I was so easily available for her, sitting so close to her, she was converted into a morph, a statue. However, finding her focus of romance in her adolescent mind, her point of attraction for bestowing love, so close, so nearby, so easily available, she got befuddled, totally perplexed. She could not decide what to do. She could think nothing to do. In my childish misgivings I was rather wondering if she would compel me that day to fulfil all her carnal and fanciful desires. The same desires, the same imaginary spectres, phantoms, that gave me nightmares regularly to think of them!

Nonetheless, I kept on teaching her as directed by her father, my preceptor; and she kept on following me obediently, betraying a mock obedience. I was not addressing her by any appellation, however, I was merely uttering the sentences from the book. I was neither paying any attention to the pronunciations she was uttering after me: whether correctly or incorrectly. If she pronounced incorrectly, my foot! I was least bothered. I was not her teacher or master! That I ought to be concerned! She was rather my enemy, my troubler, nagger! *'Nigger!'* I mused contemptuously.

We were sitting hidden near a bush at a considerable distance from the rest of the class. I would rather have liked both of us to sit somewhere beside the rest of the class, but she took me leading far away from the class, and beckoning to me she commanded: "Come, do sit here! Lest nothing should be understood in the din of the class." I hesitated a whit, but could do nothing, she was the princess of her kingly father! I complied with every command of hers. That's how slavery would have evolved, as also, how regality would have come into vogue in the society.

Amazingly for me, as soon as she settled down to study under my tutelage, she lost her elan, her self-confidence; she suddenly became self-conscious. I was surprised to see this change in her. For me, this was a unique experience, so far an unbeknown phenomenon; I had never before sat beside an adolescent girl, especially, of my own age. I was wondering at the thought that a jocose, enchanting lass who was so ever keen to prey upon a lovely lad of her age, when her prey came so close, within her grasp, and so easily, she lost her bearings, totally. She forgot that she had all along had me as an entity to aim at. I rather felt amused and relieved to observe her unabashed demeanour, her shyness, the same sort as I had felt in the wake of my having dropped down *Raamveer* back in my school. I had got rid of all fears and dread after that. I should be rid of all the nuisances and mischiefs at the hands of this naughty fairy after that day, I thought.

I can still remember that recess, that spring season, when in the class-room I was sitting alone reading something, possibly doing homework; overcautious as I was of my studies and my homework and class work. All other children – the classmates – had gone out in the sun. The girls had also left, so I was very happy and care-free: to find this environment perfectly suitable for study, to find such solitude. Completely free from classroom noise within the classroom itself!

Then came the sound of some rattle; eyes got turned towards that spontaneously. I saw both of them standing in the corner – *Raajesh and Raajeshwaree* – talking in hushed voices together and beckoning to me. Then in the tone that betrayed mischief they hailed me, "*Arvind! Arvind*! Won't you come here... beside us......?"

I was shocked even as I got scared. At first I thought that they might be wanting to tell me something, or ask me something concerning class or studies, but within no time the mind got filled with some slimy misgiving, and I hastened out of the classroom as if those two girls would forcibly catch hold of me and make love with me, and I would lose all grace in the process, that I would lose face forever before the inmates in the class, also, in the entire school.

So many times in the pre-schooling age, I had been hiding under a big straw basket (*jhaabaa)* with *Pushpaa,* my neighbouring playmate of that time, but such type of feeling or sensation I had never felt then. But what is this! *Raajeshwaree* has come closer to me, almost touching my body! She has come even much closer to me now! I move away in pique and disgust. She slips again and sits again beside me. I move away again. This time she lost her composure, she assumed her temporarily paused behaviour of jocularity, bubbliness and mischief-making, as she ever was. She blackmailed me by threatening: "I'm going to tell my father right now, *Arvind* isn't teaching me properly!" She emphasised the ending adjective that conveyed a lot.

I was shocked to hear this misplaced accusation. The pot calling the kettle black! She does not refrain from her antics!

"I'm going to tell my father right now, *Arvind* is eve-teasing me."

On hearing this, I started sweating and palpitating for a while, but soon, as though a cat had been entrapped fatally, finding no escape route, my self-respect got aroused and arose fiercely; I shouted, "Go, tell it! I can't teach you! Am I your *guru*, your tutor? Why should I teach? I'm not bound to teach you."

No sooner had I finished my rejoinder to her than we got summoned by the teacher to join our usual class. *Yogendra* came to us and asked us coupled with his villainous and mischievous smile, "Come on, *Aachaaryajee* is calling you both back!" His tone and body language seemed conveying to me, "You have missed the golden opportunity you were offered by Providence no one could ever get!"

She had already reached her father by then; we were close by only. Yet how far away we both had gone now!

"You could not teach even a single and simple lesson!" said *Aachaaryajee*, somewhat irritated but innocently, "Sit down, here....!"

And I saw that *Raajeshwaree* was chitchatting something interesting and engrossing with *Munnee – Roopwatee -* looking towards me with keen and mischievous eyes.

XXX

Table of Contents

7. Curse of Venus
Enter protagonist

It was winter. The same school in *Inaayatpur.* I don't remember if I was in class seven or six, but the sweetness of the incident I'm going to recall is still mesmerizing my mind. I am sitting alone in the classroom; the advantage to me is that the sunlight outside is able to reach my place inside. So I didn't feel the need to go out and take sun bath, although I was also the greedy lover of the rays of the sun-god – a passionate lover, a fan, an adorer! Perhaps the desire to do the sums that *Aachaaryajee* had given - the sums of mathematics - ahead of all the rest did not let me be at rest and enjoy my life. To remain at the top of the class, to maintain the identity as the superior most student in the class, all these attainments also require impatience as a compulsory ingredient of psyche. I am pretty confident that I should do the homework at school itself, for at home I have to do yet more, the tasks thought out of my own consciousness, intelligence and wisdom – all but the imagined pursuits. Nevertheless, I found that the questionnaires obtaining in the text books were quite lengthy and also difficult ones, and at certain spots the questions were intractable as well. Difficult questions, so to say! Many a time, in the process, my mind got irritated.

Be it the winter, or be it the rains, all seasons seemed alike in childhood. Even in this season of winter I was wearing half-pants, beneath which, of course, no other underwear e.g. tights etc. For this abnormality, today itself in the morning, I had become a butt of joke for the fellow classmates, a victim of their ridicule. Half-pants are inadequate to do the job for which they are put on, that is, to hide the organs of social shame, of sex and sensuality. This was also one of the causes behind my angst and irritation choosing not to go out along with the brats. To hide my self-shame!

I had no grudge against my parents for my having to put on the half-pants without any tights beneath them. For parents might not be, rather, might never be, put in dock for such shortcomings on their part, and deprivations of their wards. I was preached like that all along, everybody else is, too. Also that none of their actions or inactions, even those verging on indolence and criminality, sin or misdeed, can be dubbed as culpable crime!

Better not to even consider their actions or inactions! On the contrary, ironically, if a progeny violates this ruling, this tradition, and declares or considers as such regarding one's parents, one is declared a sinner, a criminal; he becomes a prey to the anger and displeasure of the society; he is expelled from the sphere beyond the boundary line of civility or gentility. Such is the reality of social freedom! Or of freedom of speaking truth, revealing truth! On this planet called

Mother Earth!

That's why, on the contrary, I was angry with my colleagues, for their ignorance, for their stark 'backwardness'. Why did those people laugh deriding me? Why do these people scoff and sneer at something that is not covered properly? What is there so derisive, despicable or dangerous beneath the half-pants on the slight and innocent glimpse of which so much hue and cry!

The creator has sent everyone naked onto this planet. Man unwisely covers his limbs and organs, and renders that act of covering itself expedient! Rather, uncovering the organs is called immoral and illegal! How cruel the human beings and society are! How foolish! Oh, the free-handed boon of liberation bestowed by God on living beings has also been usurped by *Manu's* children out of deviousness! Presently, every human being is obliged to cover his innate nakedness.

Covering one's nakedness or nudity entails compulsion to earn money; money implies a phenomenon which in itself is a deception, a contrivance, an injustice, a fraud, which is being perpetrated by society, by the collective consciousness of human beings, or as the author contemplates, by the throng of the populace, on the freedom of the individual, on the free consciousness of mankind. Man is obliged to earn money; money which *per se* is a dirty thing, a bad thing, incarnation of evil - *Durgunaavatar*! If one does not earn money, one would become naked or would be rendered nude in due course, which paradoxically is considered unsocial, therefore ridiculous and disgusting!

The all-pervading phenomenon of clothing and cloaking has progressed spectacularly during last one century, and also, has been progressing faster day by day, and the tendency of man to hide oneself or one's self has seen a phenomenal increase in the same proportion. What a man does not hide these days! Whatever hope remains is left with the young lasses who are shedding their clothing in the reverse proportion!

The program of my mind's computer dispenses that the organs under the half-pants should probably be kept hidden; if only for the reason that this single act would help in inculcating other disciplines in the psyche of society. In checking many an 'anarchy' if at all those actions are worthy of being called 'anarchy'! However, any event happening in the arena of Nature cannot be considered as unbecoming or anarchic.

It was time for the mid-day meal at school. There was still half the time left. I was glad to contemplate that half the homework or classwork would be finished there itself.

Suddenly,

"*Arvind!*", a hushed voice! A whisper!

I got alarmed.

My eyes were turned towards the source of voice, and saw that two teenagers – damsels of girls - were standing next to each other in the corner and pushing each other. As soon as I saw them, they shrunk even deeper into the corner, and started nudging each other. 'You say, you say!' I heard them say to each other.

What could be such a terrible thing that each one of them was ashamed of saying to me? *Raajeshwaree,* too, who looked so agile, sprightly and articulate, or at least she pretended to show off like that? And also, *Raajesh* who always seemed to be so serious and serene, ever engrossed in herself only? I got apprehensive at the quick in my mind.

In the next instant, I saw *Raajeshwaree's* tender hand waving towards me and beckoning me -- calling me towards them, and whispering from those very attractive, pink, thin lips: 'Arvind! Come here!'

Now I got clear about the intent of both the girls. But what intention? I haven't been able to decide this to this day.

With extreme alacrity and with a sense of inordinate urgency I dropped my pen and notebooks as such, and rushed out of the class-room in such a hurry as though the two arrows of the Cupid, those incarnations duo of libido – the two damsels, would catch hold of me and embrace me in their seductive arms. I could suspect in my inexperienced fancies such a danger, such an adventurous behaviour, from *Raajeshwaree*: she seemed to me so audacious even as innocent.

And my wishful thinking that I would complete the school work at school itself, thus remained unfulfilled.

However I might have considered myself victorious or having escaped by skin of a tooth, yet I noticed a bitter change in the attitude of the two lovely girls in that when I rushed out and heaved a sigh of relief finding myself amongst the melee of other lads, I had heard behind me *Raajeshwaree* hurling abusive tongue against me: '*Deeyaa Joraa! Buddhoo! Bodum!* (Worth lighting a lamp on his pyre! A buffoon! A rascal!). And later on also, she seemed to be calling me stupid.

Outside, the lads were all care-free and merry, none was aware of such serious and amorous developments going on in the desolate corners of the world and in the hearts of two opposite sexes.

I felt that after that incident *Raajeshwaree* had never again been infatuated with me, rather, she was never pleased with me. Incidentally, with this development which I was taking as my providential escape, I felt that I developed a sense of loss. I realised that the feeling of *Raajeshwaree's* liking me or loving me was acting as a psychological spur for me; it bolstered my self-esteem and sharpened my brain-power, as though. I regretted that loss forever thereafter.

Nevertheless, I could never muster courage to think that such an enamouring beauty as *Raajeshwaree* should come in contact with me or should be on talking terms with me, or should talk to me so frankly, least of all in front of other lads. I just wished that somebody should have loved me but should not have shown it before others or even to me. That one should keep one's love towards me confined to one's heart only! Paradoxically, the converse observance of the English dictum: 'If you love someone, show it!'

This way, this was the insult of that fabulous beauty – the Venus - on my part and resultantly her curse hurled upon me as a sequel even as unspoken. That was the curse for my having neglected a divine beauty, having neglected a god-send, a blessing! And this curse fructified in totem in the times to come as we would see.

XXX

Table of Contents

8. Lunar Eclipse In The Mart

Enter protagonist

First you listen to the story of *Buddhapaal*; not the tale, rather introduction. The introduction is very simple: *Raajeshwaree* lived at *Buddhapaal's* place, not as a tenant, but as an honorary tenant. Yes, the same Extension Teacher, her father, *Shri Jaageshwar Prasaad Sharmaa* hailed from a far off village called *'Doongraa Jogiyaa'*. His two teenager daughters had also come with him here to pursue their studies. *Raajeshwaree* was elder one; don't ask me the name and introduction of the younger one. I might have wished for her love, but that fairy of a lass did never make me hear her lovely words, or oblige me by throwing her slightest glance towards me. What could she have achieved even if she did? The one who mustered courage to show me her affection and love, and also, ventured so much as to talk to me, I was foolishly scared of her. I am like an audience who can only read the lesson of love, but cannot enact the role of loving on the real-life stage of the world.

Why? Because I've been taught all along since my babyhood that love, especially towards the fair sex, the women folks, is alike the black, dark, midnight leading to utter hell – hell(?). Also, that it's only the *Brahmacharya* (?) that ultimately leads to salvation(?).

By now, the discerning

readers must have guessed that *Buddhapaal* was the scion of a wealthy family even as of farmers, possessing a spacious and well-built homestead. Looking at *Buddhapaal* made one realise the veracity of the *Sanskrit* saying that a person's family background can be inferred from their scion's body. *Buddhapaal* was endowed with a very shapely and beautiful body!

I used to call him *Buddhapaal* only, but the other day something happened as follows. As usual, I was returning with my cousin, *Yuvraaj*, from school towards the village, following the path along the bank of canal. This canal virtually divided my village and the school in two disparate geographical regions. Therefore, if there were full water in the canal, then to go to the other side of the canal, one had to go to the magnificent bridges built by the British government, which were built at distances of almost three miles each. Today was such a day; it was also a Saturday!

Suddenly, I observed that my cousin stopped in his tracks. He had many a companion accompanying him, all his classmates. I was in junior class obviously.

"Look, *Yuvraaj!* Do look thither!' shrieked *Hari Baabaajee.*

I looked too. Well, *Yuvraaj* did indeed.

'Look thither, she's going there..... ' exclaimed *Hari*, almost jumping and hopping like apes; jerking his own chest, like a lumpen!

For me, this was an entirely unwarranted and untoward incident that was taking place there right before my innocent eyes. I eagerly looked towards the other shore, and found that such a splendidly dressed *Raajeshwaree* along with her equally charming and well-clad bubbly younger sister was going behind their father. *Raajeshwaree* had become utterly neglectful of me for the past few weeks; especially after that incident involving us three in the class during the recess. And also, she had assumed a countenance of perfect reticence thereafter as regards my personality or self.

"Thither! The one in front; is it?" begs *Yuvraaj* of *Hari,* the urchin, in a relatively gracious tone, possibly feigning to behave gracefully seeing me his younger and uninitiated cousin around.

"Oh no, man! that one on the rear! That pink one.... one with thin lips.... rosy cheeks.... just see how slowly and lazily she has been straddling along.... With her legs wide apart..." *Hari* was as though finding it difficult to utter the inebriated words from his foul mouth due to his mental state of dissipation. He looked like having been overtaken by the perverted mental state of cupidity.

"Her legs seem to have been

pierced apart by *Buddh Paal*, it seems; she seems to be unable to even move forward a step!... She would definitely have been impregnated by *Buddh Paal*, take it from me!.....", my cousin also seemed to be in the similar mood of depravity and incivility.

I being of younger age and innocent notwithstanding, I could not help fathom the import of the terms being uttered, like, 'legs pierced apart', '*Buddh Paal* did' *et al*. Even in the dumb and deaf conservatory or nursery of the society all these hidden meanings do get assimilated by children of their own, without even having been told.

"*Buddhapaal* was telling the other day: 'she hugs him tight taking in her arms..., she feels like butter when in arms...., she does not let go of him once in action......!' He was saying today: 'She was saying that her *Paapaa* would take them too today, that several of the nights during last week and on last many Saturdays were theirs...., their colourful nights and activities... really a lot of fun is there when crushed within your arms....!', *Hari* had almost lost sense of what he was uttering. He didn't know what nonsense and obscenity he was talking about *Raajeshwaree*. That hapless little girl living at a place away from the protection of her mother, simply for the compulsions of schooling, even though

inconsequential at that!

Yuvraaj too used to add a couple of spicy inputs to the childish and obscene revery: "First of all, it is reported, he had taken her in the sugarcane field, and then in the reed fields; as if to make her suck the sugarcane and its juice!...."

He could hardly complete his obscenity that *Hari* lost control over himself and couldn't help splutter, 'Sugarcane got sucked... Now he makes her suck the sugarcane every day....!'

'Not every day, it's not feasible physically; week by week' *Yuvraaj* quipped.

'Who cares to vouch?' resists *Hari*, 'In my view, who would not like to lick such a cream of a damsel every day?'

By then, the talks and the things had assumed the proportions of incivility and obscenity. Also, we had walked forward. *Raajeshwaree* had walked far, too, in the meantime in the opposite direction. Our shores were different and our directions were different, too.

About a beautiful teenager, rather about both the teenager sisters, whatever these lumpen urchins were uttering, made my mind utterly depressed. If a beautiful girl lives alone with her father away from her mother, should she be defamed like that, I mused sincerely!

The need and compulsion of getting education is also an

imposition of society upon the individuals just like that of money or lucre, so to say! On top of that, it's not available everywhere, beside the dwelling of the individual, quite like the money which is not affordable by everybody.

The problem is that if you don't get education, you are called uncivilized; that's another blemish! For acquiring education, be prepared to live in unliveable places and dwellings! Distasteful conditions! Stay all alone! Endure the cold! Endure the heat! Endure the precipitation! All alone! On top of that, the lustful indulgences of the young boys of the landlords, of the owners of the dwellings where one does live! Obligation to offer the oblations, the sacrifices, in the sensual fire of those entities – whether one likes it or not!

If there were a free hand for all, if the world were running by the natural laws, who would not like to have sex, to have intercourse with the opposite sex! That is the God's loaded program onto the computer of human anatomy. How are we the beings to blame for that? To add fuel to fire, there are the untenable restrictions of society imposed on this natural tendency or activity. In such circumstances, even if one ventures to tell one's predicament to someone, who would sympathise or empathise with one; rather, the chances are that one would be rebuked and hushed up instead!

This is the only offence(?) in which the punishment is first meted out to the complainant, the aggrieved party, whilst the chances mostly are that the criminal, the culprit would go scot-free!

How pitiable is the predicament of human beings that they are obliged to earn money! For which, one has to go to places what not! In the process, one has to pay not what price! In the process what abuses one does not undergo, not only sexual abuses, but also, child abuses! What amorous indulgences one has not to indulge in! Not only oneself, but also, one's progeny get to get indulged in!

Here you are! My mind got utterly upset as though something grand had shattered so abruptly and so shockingly. The same *Raajeshwaree* whom I did consider as mine in my foolish fancies, whose lovely countenance I had taken as a preserve for myself alone for watching hers and hers for mine; on that, who had not pasted one's bill-boards of unauthorised ownership and possession! Not only have they watched that face, but also, have licked that! Who has not licked that; at least in one's perverse mentality, depraved thinking! Is she really a thing to be licked? Or, is she not?

For the first time, I felt myself as common-place – quite ordinary: I am also insignificant alike all others. Would all the beauties in the world like and love just me, or choose just me? Whomsoever they find easily accessible, would be their 'beloved one'; with that only they can enact their comedietta of love and romance. In this comedietta – of romance and sensuality – there is no specific significance of any individual or any hero figure; proximity plays a prominent role, rather. Proximity is of utmost importance. Whosoever dwells in close proximity becomes the object of romance and sensuality for the opposite sex in this society of living beings. That one becomes darling spontaneously. All the actors are alike and equal in this drama of sensuality. What comes close becomes appropriate. Such is the ubiquitous ruling of the God – the ubiquitous role assigned to all and sundry without any discrimination or discretion - an all-pervasive role!

Why is this role so ubiquitous and abundantly assigned to the living beings in the world?

XXX

Table of Contents

9. Recompense For Oblations
Enter protagonist

The same *Raajeshwaree* whom I had been keeping in the cavity of my heart or within the layers of my mind so affectionately, so caressingly, was no more worth preserving there, I felt suddenly. I started smelling bad odour emanating from her image. I wiped out her equation with me from my heart forthwith – 'sinner, evil-doer!' And by labelling what not – as I was taught by my social mores (?) – I flung her out of my heart. I felt forlorn myself after that, of course. But what could I do? How could I help it? Suddenly it was discovered that the female body that I was encompassing within the layers of my mind or heart was a rotten flesh: a stale lump of flesh!

Nonetheless, my mind was not willing to believe all that: from the face, she still looked the same – so innocent and unblemished!

'No; change definitely is there in her behaviour! She has become a little less sprightly and even lesser talkative. Remains self-absorbed. Her friends do tease her, too, now for her excessive self-consciousness.'

Her references associated with *Buddhapaal* started coming to my mind. Whenever *Buddhapaal's* name was mentioned in her presence, she turned pinkish and blushed with shyness and became self-conscious. The girls did tease her all the more on that score. It appeared as though they had come to know of it all – the rigmarole of *Raajeshwaree* and *Buddhapaal*. Earlier when I used to observe all those happenings or heard all that bantering, I took them as meaningless nonsense, but now after that incident involving *Hari* and my cousin, all those things started gaining significance and having a context, a well-thought-out cause and effect relationship.

I started recalling that in the past, when the answer-sheets of the half-yearly examination were being shown to the pupils so as to make known to them their marks, *Buddhapaal* would repeatedly come to *Raajeshwaree*. He would talk to her very intimately, unusually and unnaturally affectionately. *Raajeshwaree* did feel hesitant and abashed though. Possibly he was enquiring about her scores. Her scores were not impressive, it was but natural, given her flirtatious activities. He was squabbling with the teachers for getting her scores increased: by hook or by crook. He would write marks in red ink on several pages of the answer-book and then approach the teacher with the plea, 'See, *Maassaab!* There is a mistake in totalling the marks: the total would work out this much!' And the already harassed teacher would not have time to scrutinise all that manipulation and would toe the line of *Buddhapaal* jacking up the score of his beloved. To the satisfaction of both the lovers! Fake marks, alike the spurious love! Inconsequential all the same!

Many teachers fell prey to this trickery of *Buddhapaal,* and *Raajeshwaree*'s marks were increased illegally in many question papers. I

felt bad though, but who cared! I felt depressed to think that whereas I did score so high marks by dint of my hard work, by dint of my knowledge, on the strength of my talent, there were some students – boys as well as girls – who would get increased their marks merely by cheating in the exam, or as in that case, with the help of their boyfriends, through manipulation of marks by using the red ink! This was gross dishonesty, I thought, but who cared! Even in those days!

In the market of dishonesty and cheats, only those who do the folly of treading firmly on the so-called rules of society do lag behind (fake rules). They are not aware that those rules are the outcome of the dissipation of some cunning people of social set-up, framed keeping in mind their self-interests and out of their own desire to live on the fruits of the labour of others. Has the interest of the individual, his well-being, been taken into consideration while framing those rules? Is there any social norm in which the freedom of the individual has been ensured: the freedom to live, given to the individual by God, by Nature? The populace of human beings — the so-called society — has usurped the freedom of living from the individual. Presently even as a person wishes to live, one has to live at the sweet will and according to the will of the society, by throwing to dogs one's truthfulness and by neglecting one's value system or philosophy of life.

However, what is the significance of all these marks etc that are scored in the examinations except for being the facilitators or tools somewhere in getting the admission in any school or college, or in getting a petty job somewhere, or in getting a little momentary applause from some people – only well-wishers -- as I did in my case? Yes, some teachers do make living-legends out of some students to keep themselves, their school and especially their students motivated, or mesmerised: like they did in my case long after I had left the school!

But it's all about level playing field, equal opportunities and principles as regards competition. The same rules should apply to all without discriminations of any kind whatsoever; only then can a real, true evaluation be made in a competition — whether it be a sports competition, or an examination competition, or a competition to get a job. But the travesty is that the same rules do not apply to one and all even in the examination. Intelligent, gifted and smart students always find themselves at the receiving end, i.e. as losers. Their conscience does not permit them to cheat or to resort to dishonesty at any cost. Whilst there are others who use all sorts of tactics, e.g. they cheat in exams without any qualms of conscience; they get another person to take the exam in their place — bought with the force of duress or bought for money. Mostly it's done on the strength of intimidation; the little man can be threatened. This is the only creature of Nature, i.e. human being, who is amenable to threats of fellow beings. Also, there are some people who catch hold of the examiner himself or herself, and get their marks jacked up immorally: either by paying money, or by using threats, or by using the stick or gun. What else doesn't happen here in this country – in the name of equal opportunities, or in the name of equitable competition for securing jobs, livelihood and power!

And the most shameful as well as regrettable aspect of this all is that these people who ought to be considered as big criminals by the set rules of society, are never ever considered as such, rather, on the contrary, their honour and prestige in society gets a boost. It is boasted that 'so and so managed to find out the whereabouts of the examiner and managed to get the marks hiked up by approaching the latter'. Or that so and so's father sent his orderly to the University office to get his ward's marks jacked up or mark-sheet changed, i.e. with better marks. How can these people be regarded as despicable or worthy of contempt when the same people are the officials who are vested with the responsibility to check such immoralities in the system? Or declaring a wrong-doer as criminal? These leaders, these policemen, these lawyers, these judges, these ministers, these so-called VIPs, these so-called senior officials, and so on!

But what does it matter for me and what does it matter for *Mahaarathee*? I shall still score the highest marks and what will happen at the most is that the difference between the marks of dishonest pupil and my achievement would be narrowed a whit. But *mahaarathee* is entirely indifferent - he already has very few marks anyway, entitling him to be ever in the category of those 'failed'. He does neither enjoy the patronage of any astute boy or girl-friend, nor does he enjoy the blessings of any teacher. He knows already that he has to fail, and that's only his destiny!

XXX

Table of Contents

10. Another Lady Love From My Previous Birth

Enter protagonist

Later on, *Raajeshwaree* did not look that enthusiastic or sprightly. After her landlord's son of her age having seduced or, so to say, abused her sexually she looked like a pretty flower whose petals had been plucked untimely: entirely graceless. Then she had already got disenchanted with me. I was however at ease thereafter – for she would not nag me anymore, and she didn't, too. Otherwise also, I was merely a dispassionate, adolescent youth whilst any adolescent and vivacious lass would require a stout youth who could do something, or who could give something: something tangible, something substantial, something concrete. Not a fickle minded lad like me who would only flee from the scene at the sight of a girl whether she be an adolescent, a youth or an adult lady. That's, I contemplate, the prerequisite for partaking of the drama of what we call love, libido and life.

Thus far I have been so much engrossed in dwelling on the story of *Raajeshwaree* that it might seem as if I had done nothing in life except for flirting with the girls, damsels and fairies, or except reminiscing about them only all the time. Nevertheless, that's not the case at all. The protagonist of this autobiography might have done everything else in life, but he has not indulged in those activities that are dubbed as 'bad or amorous' by human society, including the flirting with the girls at school.

But, how can I omit to reminisce the story of *Roopwatee*? She was the only one who seemed to be in love with me to the hilt and accepted no social taboo in showing her liking towards me quite openly, or brazenly, so to say. Until I left the school! She had been playing with me and nagging me till the end of my departure from that school. *Raajeshwaree*, however, had left us midway that year and returned to her native area; his father having been transferred to his native land.

Thus amongst those who nagged me or had a romantic affiliation towards me, *Roopwatee* was also one of the names, rather, the predominant name. She however looked like *Raajeshwaree's baandee* (slave or personal attendant) going by the anatomical and facial features. In fact, in the comparison of beauty and other womanly features, she would never be able to stand anywhere against a seductive and glamorous *Raajeshwaree,* of course, in my childish reckoning at that time. And this is also a fact that I had never brought myself up to liking her or having romance with her, that is, ruminate about her in my moments of solitude. In respect of the paradigms of beauty, the one who was being offered the best, why would the one go for the second best! I was in such a mood in those days! Simply a teenager's perspective! Nevertheless, I saw that *Roopwatee* persisted in her one-sided love affair with me till the end, unmindful of the fact that I liked her in the least, rather, I disliked her contemptuously, even though that was my foolishly as I realise now after so many decades.

By now, as an intelligent scholar, I had become distinguished in my class. Maybe this was why I had become the pupil of the eyes of the girls in the class and the school, if only unwillingly, on my part. I am not sure although about the causative factors! My reputation had spread all around as a rising star, as a novel constellation, rather, in the arena of scholarship or the examinations.

Those were the days of change of a season – September-October most likely. I came running home after playing outside with my playmates. My steps came to an abrupt halt in the tracks at the door! *Roopwatee!* That particle of cosmic beauty at my plaintive place! The door I was standing at was a ramshackle wooden contrivance of two or three planks. The house I was staying in was not mine; it was a 'refuge' provided us by our saviours – the brothers and sisters-in-law of our parents. It was a homestead where we were merely living hand to mouth, nonetheless oblivious of this reality, this wretchedness. *Roopwatee* was not alone. How could she be? She did not know anything about my whereabout, about my address. She was accompanied by yet another classmate of mine or hers from my own village. Not such a deal for me so far as she was concerned, nor was I for her, I presumed, at least not apparently. Seeing me, both of them smiled. But I was shell-shocked instead. The earth had vanished from beneath my two feet. I had never in my wildest dreams imagined such an eventuality occurring ever; it was such a shame in my perspective! I had nowhere to hide or dive as though, I felt. What would my mother be thinking! That her teenaged son flirted with girls of his age? 'The boy is friends with girls! At this age itself!' I was not so much as familiar with the word 'girl-friend', what to talk of being familiar with the phenomenon, the 'girl-friends'!

But why at all *Roopwatee* should have come all the way from her village – two or three kilometres away – to my village and, that too, unto my home? I was not on talking terms with her; I had never been. I couldn't recollect even a single instance when I had conversed with her or spoken even a single word to her. Nor do I have any intention as such to talk to her or have a truck with her, or love her at all. I was fretting and fuming in my heart. And why did that another girl bring *Roopwatee* to my house? If *Roopwatee* at all had been visiting hers being her classmate or friend, why she should have brought her to my place? *Roopwatee* would have asked her, I pondered over the situation. But she should have asked the former that she had no business to visit me, I being none to her. Foolish girl! This 'foolish girl' was actually in my distant relationship, of course, at this village only; the web of relationships was like that in our clan!

'If someone from my friends in the village came to notice this development! All hell would break loose. I should be defamed forever for nothing, simply for the foolishness or audacity of this girl *Roopwatee!* Oh God, what kind of calamity has this befallen my head? This girl turned out to be very shameless; how brazenly as well as unabashedly she has made it to my homestead! She is least bothered about my mother's thoughts, nor is she at all scared of her reaction. Not to speak of the shame, the decency! That can't be expected of hers!'

'Well, by God's grace my father is not here; he doesn't live in this village, he is somewhere far away – in *Veerpuraa,* as an *ad hoc* teacher, otherwise what would he have thought, had he seen this scene! He would have thought that I had become non-celibate, that I did talk to girls as well at this young age – of the teenaged!'

Talking to girls or staring or looking at them or remembering them had always been forbidden to me by my father proclaiming that as a sin:

Maatraa swastraa duhitraa vaa,
Na cha viviktaasano bhavet,
Balvaanamindriya graamo,
Vidwaansamapi karshati!
(मात्रा स्वस्रा दुहित्रा वा
न च विविक्तासनो भवेत
बलवानमिंद्रिय ग्रामो
विद्वांसमपि कर्षति!)

(Meaning thereby, one should not sit in isolation or solitude on the same seat or bed along with even one's mother, wife, or daughter, for these strong carnal senses can vanquish even the greatest scholars!)

I was most concerned about the public shame that could be incidental to this episode. If the students studying with me at my school did come to know of this affair, even as innocuous, they would not let me live in peace thereafter. They would associate my name with *Roopwatee* forever, and also, would defame me, for nothing, for no fault of mine.

Thinking of all this, of all these baseless ramifications -- and all this thinking happened within split seconds -- during moments of apocalypse the mind would be running at an stunning speed, following no norms of speed prescribed by the Creation -- I rushed into the room - running like an extremely shy girl. Even after hiding myself inside the room, I was afraid that a naughty and courageous girl as she was, *Roopwatee* who had come here all the way from her village and who had always teased me affectionately at school, might easily catch hold of me here inside this tiny room, too. I, therefore, clambered onto a small window in the wall and crouched up there within the window, or niche, so to say. From the side of the courtyard where the girls

and my mother were sitting, there was a curtain of *dhotee* (my mother's outdated *saree*) hung on a straw rope. I hid myself securely sandwiched between two thin curtains; at least I presumed that I was secure thereafter. Like an ostrich would when besieged, when chased by hounds! No doubt this was merely a sham stratagem of an ostrich in the sands of *Sahaara* desert!

By now, only my mother was holding the helm; she was bantering and talking to the two girls quite adroitly. She hailed me several times to come out unto the two visiting guests, but I didn't go outside. Then she herself got up and came to me: "Come on, you are behaving and hiding like a shy girl!"

"I won't go, I'm ashamed!" I shrank even more shyly within the small window.

"What will they think of you! What impression they would get of you! How far they have come simply to meet you?"

"I have not called them in the least!" I blurted out angrily.

"This is not the way to speak, my son!", she rebuked me and left, and again engaged the two girls in her humorous bantering. With those two lasses who were unacceptable and unwelcome to me!

"Hm, hm", my mother gruntled and added to hide her awkward situation, "He is very shy, especially of mixing up with girls!"

"No matter! Leave it! Let him be there!", this time this was the sweet voice of *Roopwatee.*

They were indulged in gossips, discussing what not on earth. Every moment of their stay at my home, that is, my shelter home, was seeming to me as if aeons were taking time to pass on.

'Oh my goodness, what if someone from acquaintances happened to visit at this time of utmost calamity and shame for me? If it so happens, I shall never be able to rid myself of the public shame associated with it. Why don't they leave here quickly? What if they themselves disclosed this shameful incident to the class, that they had been to my home the previous day? Then how shall I ever be able to show my face to anybody in public? I have nothing to do with these girls, to be true, but who would believe me, my truthful words? The world runs on the strength of gossips, grapevine and falsehoods. They would contend that if a girl didn't have any truck with me why should she have taken all the pains to traverse the rural paths all the way from her village to my village, and then to my house only specifically? And then why didn't she go to other houses, of other classmates in the same village? So many catches were there in that logic!'

A concern there was: of mine with *Roopwatee*! I now realise in hindsight. And that was *Roopwatee's* love, affection and liking for me. Category of that feeling I don't know but today at this far off distance in time when none of the actors of the play is around, neither here nor in the world in existential form, I can see that it was the same love or romance that a girl has for one's boy-friend, her lover. Alike the mythological love of *Raadhaa* with *Krishna!* Nonetheless, here the lover was a timid, shy and submissive creature, oblivious to even the sublimity of love and beauty, or rather, rendered like that during the process of one's upbringing. He would be paying for the ill-conceived notions or mistakes of his guardians or ancestors, and suffering socially as well as psychically in the process forever, throughout one's lifespan.

Today I think: what would *Roopwatee* have thought! She must have thought of me as a rascal! A buffoon! She must have got irritated and might have felt disappointed no end in her affectionate heart!

In the midst of the talks of my mother with the girls, I heard: "You will marry *Arvind,* will he still be behaving so shyly?" This was *Roopwatee*'s voice with a poser to my innately jocose, quick-witted and humorous mother.

"This is not going to happen in immediate future, but why not we marry him with you...", my mother's wittiness as well as frankness in such matters and her sense of humour was amazing and at its climax!

Hearing this remark from the mouth of my mother, I cringed like a crab within my hiding place, the hole in the wall. It fell and burst like a bombshell upon me. I was already terror-stricken and here was my mother who gave very vivid and palpable expression to my relationship with *Roopwatee!* To the inner feelings of *Roopwatee!* There was a subtle relationship between us but my mother took it to the farthest extreme of the pendulum. She made it palpable! The relationship that I couldn't understand or at least could not accept, that relationship my mother did understand, and also, did venture to formalise it, giving voice to the latent desire of *Roopwatee's* heart.

She would get me married to *Roopwatee? Ah!* How could I thereafter ever be able to show my face to anybody? There's another girl too with her; if she disclosed this fact to somebody? That my mother had proposed to establish my husband-wife relationship with *Munnee? Munnee* was *Roopwatee's* popular appellation. Once a gossip spreads, becomes a grapevine, it cannot be stopped ever, by any means. Functioning of the Creation is like that only.

"What all this are you saying!", this time *Munnee* felt bewildered and she blushed as was

ringing in her voice. She was not anguished all the same. Possibly my mother had guessed correctly about the feelings of *Roopwatee.* Unbeknown to us, probably this was the latent relationship between us that we might be harbouring in our hearts. Or, it's also true that *Roopo* would be doing all this innocently, simply for fun's sake.

After sometime when she had left, I heaved a deep sigh of relief. Still, I kept sitting there in my nook hidden, scared, for quite a while thereafter, not sure if she had actually left; for they left without much ado, without making explicit and audible noises. I was feeling a shame. Programmed humility, ingrained shyness!

XXX

Table of Contents

11. Intense Desire Of Roopwatee Fulfilled

Enter protagonist

The most obsessed lass among all the others seemed to be *Roopwatee,* the girl who hailed from the same village our school was located at, and was the daughter of a farmer, neither very wealthy nor very poor, just so-so, but an influential one, having a good deal of nuisance value, that is. And I have come to realise that nuisance value is the most effective asset in the human society. Also, he was an alcoholic, as was the wont of most of the people of martial race they hailed from in that area. For the father was from a martial race, *Roopwatee's* brother was equally abrasive and he had chosen to skip the education and devote his entire life to agriculture and farming instead, even as, he was quite young. The daughter – *Roopwatee* -- was likewise equally bold and courageous. She was quite candid as well, not at all in the habit of hiding anything or mincing words, concerning her penchant and love for me even. Openly she expressed her love towards me in the class and the school, and I, on the contrary, felt extremely embarrassed, shy as I was to see and face her overt behaviour, which in my traditional views was downright obscene, though it was not. She simply talked and did nothing beyond that.

As she had been to my house showed and proved that she had very intense feelings towards me. In her isolation and solitude, how much she would be longing for my company I cannot say. But it is said that when someone longs for someone or something it does materialise definitely, if the longing is really pure and strong. Being in the adolescent age of ten or eleven, it was not unusual that the girl would be doing all sorts of mischiefs with her anatomy in her isolation or solitude.

It was the class, I think, being taken by a teacher who was very simple-hearted. He was showing the marks of some terminal test to the students and to collect their answer-books the students had assembled around him helter-skelter; it was his fault primarily – of the teacher. Kids were kids; how could they arrange themselves in systematic manner! I included myself in the group, even as, I had been called by the teacher. I made it to the seat of the teacher. Nevertheless, some disorderliness took place and the teacher lost patience which he seldom lost. He picked and raised his smoothened as well as supple stick and started scaring the teenagers. The students scattered in all the directions unmindful of where they were headed or where they were stumbling and falling.

I was not to be spared, too. When the melee is out of control, no good sense or sanity prevails, only the madness reigns supreme; the authoritarian person opts to charge everybody without any discretion or discrimination. I too scampered to the rear and in the process, not finding time to revert, simply overturned, losing balance and control over my body absolutely, as though floating in the air. There would have been the pushes and pulls from other students, too, from behind me, from the side of the teacher's chair. But I saw myself falling down. *Roopwatee,* incidentally, was not there in the group, rather, none of the other girls was there in the crowd. *Roopwatee – Munnee –* was sitting just close to where all the lads were assembled. When I was falling down, I saw that she was just behind me. She could notice nothing when the anarchy broke loose. The lads were jumping over one another. I got a thrust from behind reinforced by the teacher's fury and I saw myself falling over *Roopwatee*, to my utter bewilderment. I tried to restrain myself but I was floating in the air, having no leverage to apply brakes to my fall. This was like fate had taken me into its hands. I fell and *Roopwatee* fell too. She spread on the floor, rather, her entire body was stretched on the floor under the thrust of rush of lads. I found myself falling over her. Her back was facing the ground and the breasts and face facing the ceiling with eyes closed in bewilderment and shock. I found myself stretched full length over her anatomy and my face just close to her soft and beautiful face. I felt extremely shocked to realise what had just happened: irreversible and inexorable. I was full length stretched over her adolescent body touching properly limb by limb. But that was none of my fault. That was the outcome of the circumstances, or the fates of us both would have had it, dispensed like that! With the speed of light I separated myself from her amidst the jeers, jealousy and derision of the class-fellows. I was

shamefaced, extremely crest-fallen in its wake. What would happen next was then on my mind!

That I had fallen over the girl who was the most courageous as well as articulate in the class and a bland one, was another cause of worry for me. What would she do now? I did not know that she could not know anything about the finer details of the incident.

I was worried about my prestige also in the class then onward, for everybody had seen me stretching over the beautiful girl in the open, under the sun. My psyche was at work very frenetically!

However, everybody seemed to be in shock. Waiting for the *Durgaa* to come to senses and for seeing her volcanic reaction. I being the wretched culprit, I was the most scared creature amongst all. I lamented why I had gone to the teacher amidst that melee of students.

Roopwatee regained her senses; she arranged herself, her clothes etc. and then just in the style of an offended -- hurt -- she-snake, she hissed venomously, "*Eh*, who was that scoundrel who fell over me?" Her face was all rage, very angry. I dreaded her wrath. I had never talked to her, nor did I like her at all. She was not to my liking as regards norms of beauty as per my conviction.

The classmates were too ready to disclose the name of the prey

– *Mahishaasur* - of the *Durgaa*. I was surmising that being good friends and well-wishers of mine they would not disclose to her the identity of the innocent culprit. But they did and did it gleefully, "It was *Arvind;* here he is!"

I had no blood in my veins, nor any respiration or inspiration left in my lungs, nor any heart-beats anymore in my heart! With head bent down I kept on sitting, waiting for the sentence that was going to be announced for my sin, the unpardonable as well as unprecedented sin! By that damsel of *Roopwatee!*

Unexpectedly, however, to everybody's utter surprise, more so for me, *Roopwatee's* countenance softened instantaneously on learning of this development. To everybody's surprise, not only mine! Had she been angry and calling me names I would have been much happier, for then nobody would associate her name with me, but now, she had shown her love towards me, and I had become the point of jealousy for everybody in the class all the more.

She smiled enchantingly and looking towards me said, "Oh, very sad! Did you get hurt? Are you?" To the derision and jeers of the class-fellows. They added, "Yes, yes, he fell upon you deliberately; no one else did; and he chose to fall upon you. Had he not willed to do this deliberately, why did he not run towards where other lads were fleeing?" etc.

"No, tell me. Are you hurt? If you are hurt I can give you my *chunaree* (scarf) or I can tear off a piece of it, and you can tie wherever you have got hurt." etc.

She spoke in so many words and kept on sympathising with me for quite a while. As if not me but she had fallen upon me and got hurt!

Upon getting up, I recalled, she had commented, "Who was the scoundrel who fell upon me? He was very heavy by the way!" And she had added one or two invectives in her tongue to add spice to that acerbic tongue. In that backdrop now I was finding her behaviour quite affected one. I felt as though she was longing for this episode and this pose to happen with her involving me in her dreams for long; and the intensity of her longing had made the episode a reality. Her desire had been fulfilled as though! She knew she would never get me as her life partner, but in real life she had at least once slept with me, just like husband and wife sleep with breaths intermixed and cheeks close by.

She felt relieved and satisfied as though having accomplished everything; however, I was shame-faced. I had no such longing. I longed for celibacy all along and to keep aloof from the fair sex. Such was my upbringing, though faulty one, now I realise.

As against my apprehension that I would be a butt of joke for my class-fellows thereafter given the bizarre pose I had taken with my class-fellow before the eyes of everybody, no such thing happened fortunately thereafter. Everybody let that go to oblivion, except a few bullies whose job it was to only think ill and to envy others for the latter's good luck.

XXX

Table of Contents

12. I Beat A Bully With Scale In The Class

Enter protagonist

Once while conversing with us kids, and with the presence of our father and elder uncle around, our grandfather mentioned shockingly for me that it was tough for handsome boys and pretty girls to study in the schools or lodge in the hostels. That would have been true in his school days as well, I mused, for in my own school I was being tormented and teased by bullies, definitely of somewhat older age. And I now think that I was foolish enough not to bring their bullyism to the notice of either the teachers or my parents. I was already tormented by the one-sided love-making of the petty girls towards me! Now this malady of dealing with bullies! They were those lads who were slow-minded, possibly from poor backgrounds as was evident from their gloomy and patchy dresses.

They could not compete with me in academics, so they vented their ire by teasing and tormenting me. Moreover, I was being loved by the girls in the class so overtly! That was an added salt getting sprinkled on the bruises of such vile fellows.

There were not many of such sort, but there definitely were; and my fault was that I was supposing to tackle all that menace on my own self. They were strong-bodied. They tried to crush my skull between their palms complaining that it was the skull that contained that precious gem called brain that was so sharp in my case that they abhorred. How could I help it! Sometimes they pricked my skin or nipped me when the teacher would be around, or in the circumstances when I would be embarrassed in front of others. Though I had a very high goodwill, still the embarrassment was a thing that could not be helped, nor tolerated.

Paradoxically, in my mind, I thought that my father himself was sort of a bully, and also, that if I brought the fact of nagging by those boys to the notice of my father, he would set everybody right including the teachers. That might be my fanciful thinking but I had that firm conviction at that stage. And exactly that was the reason why I did not want to take that harsh a decision, that of notifying my father in this behalf. I tried to tolerate and to make trivial of the nagging by the bullies for years together.

However, once when the answer-sheets were being shown by a teacher, and we were assembled around him in a haphazard manner, a bully tried to trouble me. He was pricking my ears from behind. When I could not tolerate anymore, I picked my wooden scale that I was holding, and struck it forcefully on the bully's arms. The strokes resounded in the class. Everybody was agape. It was obvious; it was me. Holding the ruler in hand and with eyes enlarged, enraged!

I yelled angrily, "Come! Come on!"

The teacher looked at me sympathetically but said nothing. He could guess that I had struck the bully when the limit had been breached. The bully retreated grieving in a mock drill, but did not retaliate; maybe due to the presence of the teacher. To my utter surprise, of course! I was rather preparing to flee, in case he ventured to strike me again. But nothing of that sort happened. I felt emboldened thereafter.

"This is too much!" I yelled again.

Who was at fault, everybody knew.

Surprisingly, the girls, my one-sided ladyloves felt pleased at this action of mine. Action of bravery! No beauty loves a coward!

Everybody likes a bold person. Nobody likes a meek and weak person. Violence and revenge are not all that bad as these are made out to be. Entire Creation is witness to such violent retaliations by small and vulnerable creatures.

In fact this bully was the younger cousin of our Principal, the Head Master. Yet I did not flinch from beating him. For my father was all the more stronger. And fiercer as I felt. Moreover, I had my elder uncle as a teacher in the school, that was an added protection against any pecuniary action that would have been taken against me.

The stamina, strength and resourcefulness in that sense are very essential to survive on this planet. Those who rely solely on the tenet of non-violence do suffer miserably at the hands of scoundrels and bullies.

In the class in our standard, in fact, we had two sections. The section I was in was considered to be the section of duffers, whereas the other section was the section of bright students. Paradoxically, I despite being the brightest student of the class was in the section of supposedly duffers, the lesser gifted ones. And amazingly, too, the son of our Head Master, the Principal, and his cousin of our age, of course, were in my section only. I could never fathom this mystery. In fact that was by chance, and there was nothing by design to ensure all this arrangement this way. And providentially, the lovely girls were, too, all in our section only. So despite the other section being proud of and quite often bantering about their section's superiority in respect of preponderance of brilliant students, my presence in the section of duffers or mediocre was more than enough to recompense the lacunae in the field of brainpower of my classmates. And my classmates were proud of me and they did not flinch from taking pride in this fact by articulately expressing their views to this effect.

Whereas the Principal's son was my friend, his uncle – the cousin of the Principal – was sort of a bully, big-bodied, yet slow of mind, was my enemy. This was he whom I beat with the blow of the ruler.

With this episode having taken place, actually other bullies were put on guard, too. They stopped nagging me virtually. For they had now realised the potential for violence in the prey, i.e. in me. The Nature has devised like that and the creatures living on the planet must not overly emphasise on sticking to non-violence foolishly even when violence is warranted as a natural reaction for the sake of survival of existence and protection of prestige.

XXX

Table of Contents

13. Never Go Near The Devils

Enter protagonist

His name was not *Bholoo* in any case. His mother had died when he was merely an adolescent, and his father had died much earlier than that. *Bholoo* was deaf of hearing, but not dim of intellect or wisdom, *Bholoo* meaning shorn of intellectual faculties notwithstanding. This world, rather, the human society, is so complex that it may render anybody whatever shape it likes to give one. The substance of this creation is beyond comprehension of even the conscious idols which abound it or which are made of its substance. Everybody has got one's own priorities, everybody has got one's own centres of trouble or instigating centres, so to say. Also, it's only the inconsistencies of life, the difficulties, the intractable questions, that give impetus to life and prove to be its dynamics. Moreover, no one else might comprehend the true meaning of the difficulties and agonies of others. Therefore, everybody interprets the sufferings of others in one's own way.

Bholoo's mother was childless. I don't know why, in this society, there is an evil practice of looking down upon a sterile woman – a woman who does not beget issues or who cannot. Whereas, in my view, what this country needs the most today is just the same sterile women. The sterile women, the childless women, or even the parents without children should be treated with utmost respect, rather. It is they in fact who are not overburdening the earth with the ever ballooning human population.

It can be assumed safely that there would have been once upon a time the time of violence, looting and chaos all around when every settlement or village would have had a separate ruler, the king, called by whatever name depending upon the lexicon of the geographical area. No single ruler was there who could rule the entire mass of land. People of one geographically small region did not usually obey the ruler hailing from any other geographical region. The so-called king, the ruler, was nothing but what we call the goons or the Mafiosi nowadays; he used to be synonymous with the super hooliganism. He used to make rules to suit his own whims, fancies and evil tendencies. He used to make one group of inhabitants confront with the other group on this phony pretext or the other. He subjected a large chunk of populace to be cut or chopped off in this way; and this cycle continued throughout the cycles of time, irrespective of seasons or weathers.

That is why there was dearth of humans, especially men at that time. There was a shortage of this species called human. And who else other than a woman could make good this deficiency of living beings, for she only has the ability to procreate the living beings, conscious beings from the inanimate substances of the mother Earth. That is why the title of *Jagat-Jananee* (the procreator of entire creation) is bestowed upon her so fittingly! She is rightly an object of worship, adoration, an object of reverence! That is why in those days when the woman would be sterile she would be looked down upon with contempt and hate. An object of utter derision! How else could a fruitless tree be seen in times of famine?

But presently, the circumstances are entirely different; the population is bursting forth at seams. The creatures of all the species as though have been getting birth as human species after dying there! Also, they are behaving here in the human birth as per their past tendencies of insects, animals, reptiles and beasts etc.! They could not forsake their *sanskaars,* the conditioning.

The world is still perched on the verge of chaos. The concept of order, of social life, is failing. The concept of organisations or institutions is beginning to seem as an utter mistake, an aberration. The individual's own 'self' has precluded every other consideration. Dishonest people are converting the public wealth and property into their personal property, whether by means of dishonesty or by means of scandals. Without any qualms of conscience whatsoever!

Bholoo's own mother had no financial wherewithal or social security available as such. On top of that, she was childless! Who would support her body in case of illness or emergencies? She would think. Who would help her push her life on in her old age, if at all she would live that long; although chances of her living long were very bleak. With this perspective, whatever and howsoever an underdeveloped, uneducated and unlettered mind could think one thinks and takes decisions. In gospels, too, the child has been described as the only means to take one's life beyond the horizon of death.

I, as such, was not present at that time with this body and with this consciousness in this world; my grandfather was. He used to tell jocularly quite often as to how *Bholoo's* gullible and wretched mother had undergone umpteen number of hypocrisies and performed *karm-kaandas* simply to get a son. Also, how she had stayed with so many types of so-called and sham sages and mendicants! What untoward and unbecoming activities she had not indulged in! To have a child, to have a son, specifically! Towards this end, she had squandered a larger chunk of whatever wealth she did possess as her inheritance.

Ironically, when the issue was born to her – a son – there was nothing left to nurture it. She could not afford even the costs of his schooling. Her husband had left for heavenly abode leaving the child in the womb itself. Possibly not standing the shock to think how her wife got impregnated whereas he himself was a certified sterile man! How could Nature perform such unscientific miracles? Can there be any other method also other than the natural process of procreation for begetting living creatures?

Neither there is any other process other than that of intercourse of a male and a female – whether it be of human beings or any other beings – for begetting conscious world, nor is there any violating the scientific rules, that is, nature's rules. Scientific rules are but Nature's immutable rules only! But *Bholoo*'s mother had already fulfilled that Natural prerequisite by sleeping with a male entity, of course, violating the social injunctions. However, the social set-up provided that much leeway in its rulings in the form of such hypocrites who claimed that they could bless the sterile ladies with issues.

Ironically, when *Bholoo* came of age, her mother also passed away leaving the little child in the lurch. A wretch!

And *Bholoo* was left all alone! To fend for himself!

And how about me? Listen to my experience with *Bholoo*.

As I have claimed, I have ever been a recluse, ever hesitant to mix up with people or to converse with people: of even males, not to speak of fair sex. I seldom participated in any games or sports being played by my mates, or children of my age.

It so happened one day, nonetheless, that having tired myself of studies, I ventured out for a walk or outing, so to say. For refreshing my tensed mind, my frayed nerves. Moving only a few steps away, I noticed that in the *Chaupaal* (sitting or gossip room, which was given the farcical appellation of *Kaanoon-Kotharee* by us) of *Bholoo,* there were congregated a coterie of elders who were beating summer time by playing cards. That was nothing unusual; that was a normal scene at that *Chaupaal*. Rascals and scoundrels quite often assembled there. I never played cards. Still I wished, with the intention of relaxing the mind tired of studying, that I should have a look at what was happening there. My mind wanted to enjoy the experience of certain so-called bad deeds. I went and stood up beside the card-playing people. Card game! Dishonesty is also a game, huge entertainment! People were dishonest among themselves too, so-called 'upper caste' people as they were. I stood beside the players without any intervention or intention. Game of cards it was! A game of gambling, of cheating! Cheating is *per se* a game, too. A big game; a tremendous source of entertainment. Those elders were indulged in cheating with one another. I was simply standing there as a mute spectator, merely chuckling once in a while, now and then.

Bholoo was probably losing the game or money. He was off mood. I don't know what made him think that I had stolen his cards. He pounced upon me all of a sudden. I ran away in fear. Seeing me running in fear, *Bholoo* misconstrued it as the vindication of his suspicion that I had hidden or stolen his cards. He ran fast, too, to chase me, to recover the imaginary cards. I ran away screaming piteously like a calf as if chased by a wild wolf. In that process, I however realised how terrified a victim must be feeling when being chased by a hunter, and how even an innocent person could be made victim of suspicion and, in turn, might be intimidated, beaten, persecuted and punished.

I was running away screaming and calling for help. From God, as though! That day I realised, too, that God indeed comes to the rescue of innocent ones.

Fortunately, my elder cousin, who was very strong and stout, was sitting at a distance nearby only talking to one elder of the village, and there only my father too was sitting. I saw some ray of hope.

They however could not understand the bizarre situation for a while, and did not react immediately.

When they realised the situation and saw my condition as well as predicament, they came into action to save me from the villain – the rascal *Bholoo*. My cousin chased us both. Still I kept on running because *Bholoo* was still running fast and was in very angry mood. Had he caught me in that state of mind he would have thrashed me without any fault of mine and would have thus earned a huge amount of evil deeds. Evil deeds, of course, he kept on earning otherwise too, off and on. This was no unusual thing for such a habitual scoundrel.

And by the time he got sense he would have hit me, so I was running away. The beast never seeks a reason for its violent as well as unjustified actions!

Confronting the animal or a beast, a sensible person ought not to reason with it, rather, one ought to run away from it as fast as one could. *Bholoo* at that time was nothing short of an animal, a beast, absolutely beastly!

But God came quickly to my rescue sensing my utter innocence and piety; and before I could fall prey to *Bholoo's* nefarious hands, he had fallen prey to the lion-like hands, rather, paws of my cousin. Alike a cow guffawing in the claws of a lion! He fell down with a thud on the ground. I became so happy, and felt so relieved! He was now sneering and entreating like a person on the gallows. In that state of mind I realised the significance of stamina, strength and power for survival on this planet.

The condition that I would have been in, had I fallen in his hands, was now *Bholoo's* condition. It seemed as if *Narasimha*, the mythological incarnation, had come to my rescue from nowhere to protect me from the torture of mythological *Hiranyakashipu!* The *Narasimha* must have emerged like this only by tearing apart the pillar – to kill *Hiranyakashipu*, to safeguard the pious *Prahalaad*. The existential implication of the mythological tale is exactly the same: when the cruel king *Hiranyakashyap* who was a *shraman* king, the follower of Lord *Buddha,* and practitioner of *Vipashyanaa,* got angry with his son – *Prahalaad* - who believed in idol worship, particularly, of Lord *Vishnu* – he tried to kill *Prahalaad* by striking with his sword; however, the sentry standing nearby beside a pillar, out of pity and compassion for the little child, the young prince, came to the latter's rescue and killed the king. For he acted like a lion, the proponents and supporters of prince *Prahalaad* hailed him as the *Narasimha*. Whoever gets the chance to write the history writes it with one's viewpoint in prominence.

My heart was very terrified; it was beating very fast. I lost faith in the dictum and belief that everything happened through a cause and effect relationship. I was absolutely innocent, yet I was suspected and chased by a would-be marauder.

That's exactly why some people lose faith in the existence of God. I too sometimes lose faith in the existence of God. In His Creation – this world - there are countless such errors, not one or two! Some incidents have nothing to do with any reason, they seem to be taking place without any reason. God is a bully boy! God is a naughty boy! I thought in my childish angst against *Bholoo*.

Well, when my cousin brought that rascal *Bholoo* to his knees, the spectators at the scene who did not know the background of the incident set off decrying my cousin who was innocent, accusing that he had raised hand on his uncle; for *Bholoo* was his uncle by distant relationship. When we explained the situation and proffered my similar innocence, they got pacified to some extent but wondered why I should have run away instead of clarifying my stand to *Bholoo*. But childhood does not have all those skills at that age, and suffers for no fault of it, in turn. That is why childhood is called a hell, in the eyes of enlightened ones. Totally helpless! At the mercy of rascals and scoundrels called grown-ups and adults! Parents not

excluded definitely!

XXX

Table of Contents

14. Dwarfism Of Masters

Enter protagonist

We were inside our classes, studying sincerely, our teachers being all busy teaching us. All of a sudden, we heard loud voices emanating from the throats of two elders; not elders but the teachers. The serene routine of studies abruptly came to a standstill. All eyes were turned outwards, peering through the doors and windows of the rooms. Already those windows and doors were without any grills or covers, without any planks put on them. This sort of occurrence was unheard of, and also, unexpected of the elders, least of all the teachers.

We observed that two middle-aged men were indulged in altercation and squabbling. Out of curiosity, all the children started coming out and watching the unimaginable spectacle unfolding out there before their eyes.

Lo, there in that sprawling space, near the teachers' staffroom, they were quarrelling in loud voices, at the highest pitches, not refraining from even using the foul language, unbecoming of those elders or the teachers, in front of the formative, sensitive, minds of the kids, the school going kids. They were using disrespectful slangs against each other. In fact, one of them was the

Manager or the virtual owner of the school whilst the other one was a teacher of the school, however, both hailing from the same village and curiously related ones, as well. Teacher, of course, was a highly qualified one, at least that was the impression given us by the grown-ups, and also, through the grapevine. The Manager was a man whose eyebrows were ever warped; he was never seen in a good mood or wearing a pleasant countenance. At least he could never smile; that was my impression, and that was the conclusion of most of the kids!

"They are so aged, still they are squabbling! They are teachers and they are fighting! In front of those children whom they always preach: 'not to fight, not to quarrel, not to use foul language!' And they themselves are doing all those things! Travesty of schooling system and sham precepts! We kids were wondering.

When teachers – masters – themselves were fighting obscenely, how could they preach or teach others the lessons of peace, decency and civility? What right they would anymore have to tell the kids that the latter ought to behave with others with affection and peace?", *Mahaarathee* was mumbling, I noticed.

We saw that with the passing of time, and as the gathering of spectators swelled, the tongues of both of them became all the more acerbic and abusive. They were using abusive language, foul language, obscene language, the lexicon that normally emanates from the womb of utter dejection and frustration. The abuses emerging from the core of their subconscious stratum! That betrayed the reality of the hypocrisy they showed towards each other in normal and formal dealings.

Abuses have no meaning. Nevertheless, those nonsensical words, how hurtful they seemed! How injurious they were proving in effect for the sensitive and innocent minds and hearts of the kids! That quarrel! Those abuses! Coming as they did from the foul mouths of two supposedly responsible as well as respectable teachers! From the lotus-mouths of *gurujans!*

"How crazy and hypocritical everything is! They lose their right to preach anybody anymore to the effect that one should maintain peace and should behave decently. This incident, this scene, shears them of the right to be fitted in the dictum: *Aachaarya Devo Bhava!"*

Perhaps there could not have been a more bitter and ugly fight between two sensible and responsible persons. That too in front of the whole school! In front of all the kids! As has already been said by the old people, the wise ones, in this type of conflict, often the side which has already a liberal image in the psyche of the spectators does get the sympathy of the audience, whereas the side whose image is made of an autocratic person in the psyche of the spectators becomes a victim of the audience's irreverence.

Most of the students had voices and opinion against the school manager – they were not mincing words in expressing their adversarial opinions against him. The school manager *Raajpaal Singh* was a pedigreed *Thaakur* (feudal scion)! A very dislikeable and irascible soul! He had an image of an irritable minded person. Most of the children felt frightened by his presence, getting scared of going in front of his eyes.

The result was that every tongue in the school was wagging against *Raajpaal Singh* and his imagined vices, and eulogizing the virtues of *Malkhaan Singh* on the contrary.

The fallout was what could have been: the next day, a management meeting was called. We – the children – were curious and were peering hither and thither and trying to listen and ascertain the next outcome of the intriguing episode. From the room where the meeting was taking place loud voices could be heard coming out.

Although the snake of feudalism was supposed to have been long dead, yet the tone and tenor of the voices that were emerging from

the walls of that room were testimony enough to betray that the feudal snake was still hissing and raising its hood. It was the year of 1969 or 1970; it had hardly been 20 years since *Zamindaaree* system had been abolished in the country. The people who thrived in that system were still alive. The generation was still alive which had put on the fabricated garb of *Zamindaaree,* but did not want to take it off despite having been shorn of their position and prestige in the novel dispensation of governance. The garb had become rags, torn, dirty, but there were people who were not letting it go. Truly, old habits die hard! Therefore, the voices that were rising from that meeting room were indicative of the fact that feudalism was not yet dead. *Raajpaal Singh*'s side was strong, whilst that of *Malkhaan Singh* was weak, because he was weak in the order of the so-called family pedigree, even as, not so weak. The decision of the jury went against him.

Malkhaan Singh was fired from his teaching job because he had done the unpardonable offence of insubordination towards his bosses; moreover, because he had used abusive language against *Raajpaal Singh,* the Manager, the virtual owner. Abusive language did *Raajpaal Singh* as well use during the heat of arguments, but he was the Manager, also, the owner of the school. And in line with established beliefs, an owner has every right to peel off the subordinate's skin, more so, in the feudal set-ups! The wretched servant, the poor man, has no right to resist or protest, nor should he dare resist! He'd better keep putting up with everything, with his head bowed down, even if the owner, the petty creature, the fake human being, did make him to suffer no matter howsoever pathetically. So *Malkhaan Singh's* sin was that he had the audacity to protect his self-esteem, that he had made full use of his conscience, without caring for the palpable fact that however brilliant and highly educated he might be, he was after all merely a servant, and that a servant had no other duty but to suffer all sorts of tortures at the hands of one's masters. No matter whether the masters be scoundrels or whatever!

Nonetheless, the unwise and apparently high-handed action of *Malkhaan Singh's* expulsion from the school assumed the shape of a scandal, as if somebody had disturbed the hive of stinging wasps or buzzing bees. The meeting finally was dispersed. The congregation of agitated boys had assembled outside the meeting room; everybody got to know of the saddening news. *Malkhaan Singh* was their favourite as well as affectionate teacher; how could they let a person not at all at fault be punished so brazenly, so unjustifiably!

Malkhaan Singh put on the cloak of martyrdom within no time. His elder brother was accompanying him, too. All the boys congregated around those two simple-looking and perceptibly innocent or, so to say, victimised souls. They were all sheltered under a *Shireesh* tree. *Shireesh* is an evergreen tree; it never sheds its leaves and is never seen devoid of leaves. Unbeknown to the assemblage, it assumed symbolism at the moment.

The mental condition of both the brothers was that of martyrs. In fact the spur on which the events had taken such a distasteful turn was apparently trivial, merely the late coming of *Malkhaan Singh* that day, and *Raajpaal Singh's* rightfully pointing it out to the erring teacher. For such a trifling issue, so much ado was made! That's typical of human race! Ego! Clash of personal egos! One craved for subjugating the other, whilst the other was not willing to be subjugated.

The boys assembled around, particularly, those who considered themselves to be bullies amongst the gathering, started getting restive. The embers of rage set off smouldering gradually. They were explicit in voices of their criticism of the decision taken, and were mincing no words; even as, they were standing at stone's throw from the meeting venue. Some of them even chanted the refrains such as: *Taanaashaahee naheen chalegee! Saamantshaahee naheen chalegee!* ('Dictatorship won't do! Feudalism won't do!')

Nevertheless, no step should advisably be taken without first devising a well thought out strategy and its variants in case of its eventually flopping. *Malkhaan Singh* himself and his brother seemed to be votaries of this ideology; they were repeatedly emphasising this fact before the restive melee of the students. They advised the boys to be silent in *Malkhaan Singh's* own interest.

The members of the meeting came out with their heads held high, some of them, of course, even arrogating themselves as erstwhile *zameendaars.* Some had sadness betrayed across their countenances at the outcome of the meeting. The boys got excited to see those who were arrogating. To these fresh sprouts of humanity what intrigued the most was the showiness, the hypocrisy, the artificiality of the adults. They loved natural, spontaneous, demeanour on the part of fellow human beings. The votaries of the Manager were all arrogant and it was perceptible from their behaviour, particularly, after having taken a myopic decision. They were nonetheless not aware of the imminent storm that was to follow their decision. Little did they know that there would be many supporters of the other side, particularly, from the student community, who would flout their decision so brazenly.

I also walked my way to the village. And my smooth path was along the canal. One had to walk a long distance on the bank of the canal before taking a turn towards the village through a bridge. Almost on the same route to a great length, that is, along the canal, *Malkhaan Singh* also used to go to his village; and incidentally, *Raajpaal Singh's* village was also *Malkhaan Singh's* village, that is, *Rakheraa.* So the troupe that had come in favour of *Raajpaal Singh*, riding a small passenger-friendly bullock cart, *Rehaloo*, was also now going back to *Rakheraa*, and by taking the same – solitary -- route. Many other boys from the supporters of *Malkhaan Singh* were also accompanying me that day along the canal – making plans, conspiring against the arguably wily manager. *Malkhaan Singh* and his brother were also travelling with us students. They were having their bicycles, we lads were pedestrians as ever, so the brothers duo chose not to ride us past on their bicycles; they rather chose to walk with us. The atmosphere got highly charged at that moment! Naive boys were agitated, not that they had any genuine sympathy towards *Malkhaan Singh*, but because they were finding an opportunity to usher in *'Inquilaab'*, as did everybody during the freedom movement. They were not there during that opportune time of national movement, however, presently it was an opportunity for them to assume martyrdom of a sort, for a cause. Logic nevertheless behind the *'Inquilaab'* was amiss!

'We will take revenge! We'll get you restored to your job at school again! Dictatorship will not work! .....', angry voices were bursting forth.

In the meantime, the *Rehloo* of those feudal lords appeared to be coming from behind us on the bank of the canal. The boys got excited. Violence is the first symptom, and also, the consequence of senseless rage of the masses. A naive mind takes excitement unto violence – that seems to him a spontaneous recourse. But a sound mind does not let the rage metamorphose into violence – it does not even touch the violence – it rather converts its energy of agitation into creativity; he uses it to increase creativity. Just alike nuclear energy, that converts the destructive tendency of subatomic particles into the creative tendency, the energy -- the electricity.

Malkhaan Singh genuinely as well as advisably tried to pacify the boys and entreated them sincerely, "This should not be done; I am walking with you people, everything will come upon me, I shall be blamed for your actions."

That notwithstanding, as soon as the *Rehaloo* of *Rakheraa* approached us, the boys started shouting slogans with an intention to show off, to express their anger: *'Inquilaab Zindaabaad!* Dictatorship will not work! We will take revenge!.....' *et al.* Some mischievous ones even threw dust towards them. For a while, an ugly scene was created, an awkward situation was created. People sitting in the *Rehloo* were also shocked; they had not suspected such a reaction from supposedly impartial kids. How could they? That was a rural scenario, unwary of such things as reaction or revolution, leave alone *'Inquilaab'* etc. What sort of reaction this was! More importantly, why it at all was! In their feudal mind-set, and social structure, such a scene was unimaginable, in a way unlikely. They could not understand these wonderful traits and nuances of the novel system called democracy as yet. Could anybody, least of all these teenaged boys, dare misbehave with those feudal relics in this manner or so contemptuously in their heydays? Well, the defiant boys were assuaged, and good sense prevailed upon them, even as, they also agreed.

When *Rehloo* had gone ahead, at a safe distance from those boys, and eventually, the boys had taken a turn towards our village, the riders realised to their utter shock that the boys hailed from *Maar-Haraa* village, a village of their feudal peers. My grandfather used to narrate so many tales of their friendship with the lords of *Rakheraa.*

Having come to realise this fact, one of them commented loudly from the farther going vehicle, "Dear chaps, we didn't expect this from your village! There have been very close relationships between our two villages ever...."

Sheer blackmail! Emotional blackmail! Blackmail of the feelings of young hearts and minds! However, I got catapulted into the past, reminiscing the multitudes of tales my grandfather kept on reeling out concerning his feudal friends, the *zamindaars* of *Rakheraa* and *Chingaraavalee,* as to how the latter kept on coming frequently to ours and we in turn kept on visiting their villages.

XXX

Table of Contents

15. Rustic Love Affairs

Enter protagonist

Now turning to our homestead, the strife that characterised the adults at school also typified my parents; they were ever quarrelling; rather, it would be better to say that my father always kept on creating the atmosphere of strife and tension in the homestead. He was alike a hearth, a fireplace.

Husband and wife are supposed to be in love affair, but I noticed continually that it was just the converse in respect of my parents.

However, there was no dearth of love affairs between lads and lasses in our hamlet. In seventh

standard, I noticed that this factor of the society made itself apparent to me very eloquently. And in this respect, my mother too involved me in those slimy affairs by making me read the intercepted love letters. Shamelessly, to my mind!

I noticed that many love affairs were going on those days in our immediate vicinity in our village. How many other such affairs were going on in the entire village I could only surmise! One such affair was going on between *Devraanee buaa* and *Veerendra,* and the other one was being played between *Kaunsaa Buaa* and an anonymous yet not-so-young a lad of our neighbourhood. There were reasons behind the flowering of these love episodes between these pairs. As for *Devraanee Buaa,* she was the middle daughter of *Pradhaan Chaachaa,* the same prodigy who was a favourite recourse of my father in respect of every conceived domestic calamity for the latter; also, the same fellow who had been involved in the slimy affair with the mother of *Veerendra* as described in earlier chapters. On the other front, *Kaunsaa Buaa* was actually *Kaushalyaa Buaa* and was a buxom beauty, hailing from a well-to-do family by the standards of our village. And it is well-known to everybody that the sexual tendency had a direct link to the diet and the financial standard of a family. One who eats well masturbates well, or coagulates well with the opposite sex. The boy with whom she was seen sleeping at various odd places was actually having his abode beside that of the girl. And it is the tendency of human clan that whenever a woman and a man reside in proximity they tend to fall in pornographic relationship if only unintentionally, out of corporeal or biological tendencies. And they did. The same natural law acted in respect of *Devraanee buaa*; the mother of *Veerendra* frequented the residence of *Pradhaan Baabaa* and Veerendra as a young lad accompanied his mother to her paramour's house. Initially, the younger age protected him from sexual inducements, but gradually and definitely, the same age factor when it grew older led him to fall in objectionable sexual relationship with the daughter of his mother's lover. In a sense, the feeling of avenging his mother's fouling at the hands of *Pradhaan chaachaa* might be working unconsciously on the youth's mind.

Veerendra used to write titillating love letters to the youthful lady. Here, it is worth notifying that actually both the pairs of lovers derided or accused one another for their love-making. They decried the affairs of the other pair, however, not minding their own slimy dissipation. Since *Devraanee* used to spread the slanderous news about the affairs of *Kaunsaa* and the lad, *Kaunsaa Buaa* too spied on the affairs of *Devraanee*

and *Veerendra* constantly. Not only she, at times, others too intercepted the love letters exchanged between those lovers. One such interceptor was the cousin of *Devraanee*; her name was *Deshraanee*, the same girl who slept at our house to give company to my mother and us during our father's absence.

She kept on intercepting the love letters exchanged between *Devraanee* and *Veerendra* and to relish their contents she shared the contents of the letters with my mother, too. My mother was not averse to relishing such slimy affairs, a free-style living as she had enjoyed in her parent's house and village.

I could sense all such things and their hushed voices going on around me and around my house, for I was not that innocent, and moreover, I had myself been subject to such tyranny on the part of my 'Bhaisaahab', the child abuser, the rapist. However, still I supposed that those lady adults would not let such things spill to my level, and that they would respect my assumed innocence.

But one day, when I reached home from school, after giving me food, my mother called me in the room and handed me a piece of paper. I shuddered even before I could open it and read its contents. Immediately I realised that it was the love letter of one of the pairs of loving birds. It was! It was the letter written by *Veerendra* to *Devraanee.* My mother asked me to read it for her; she was unlettered, she could not decipher it. Somehow she had come across this letter. I hesitated. But my mother insisted on my reading the sexy and pornographic letter. I read it hesitatingly, for its language was very passionate and sensuous, which was indigestible to my adolescent tastes. So far I had assumed that an adolescent and a young man ought to shun all such things and affairs. But here was a mother herself, my own mother, who was making me read an obscene and pornographic stuff. I felt shocked, the same sort of shock I had had when my *'Bhaaisaahab'* had abused me, an innocent child.

When I had finished reading and felt crestfallen once more, as if to add insult to injury, my mother offered me a piece of advice, too, in the field of love-making and courting of the young lasses; she said, "If at all you intend to love a girl and engage her in the affair, first throw a small pebble or piece of stone at her; if she responds favourably, you may feel safe and go ahead."

I was doubly ashamed. However, my mother was not. As if such affairs were nothing abnormal, as if those were quite natural things in the scheme of Nature!

Later on, one day, we found *Kaunsaa Buaa* rushing to our house in a very happy mood and disclosed gleefully to my mother that

Devraanee Buaa had aborted a child.

My mother enquired how she knew. She further expounded, "There is blood stream flowing in the water channel, the drainage, coming from the residence of *Devraanee.*"

My mother kept mum.

I was present there and they did not mind that factor at all. For them their own sensual pleasures had primacy over the sensibilities of an adolescent lad of twelve.

Our refugee house was towards the fringe of the village, having its door towards the fields, the wilderness. And the house or huts of the lad *Kaunsaa Buaa* had been having affair with was towards that side only. I had sighted *Kaunsaa Buaa* gesticulating sensuously towards the boy from outside our house, shamelessly and unashamedly. Sexual sensation is such a powerful phenomenon that minds no shame, no norm, no social prohibition., The same *Kaunsaa Buaa* used to be seen sleeping with the sturdy boy at several odd places, like, inside the hay-stacks, the cow-dung-cake dunes, the ruins of abandoned buildings and, of course, the crop fields where it was free for all without any risk of being detected.

The other day, nevertheless, when I came back from my school, I found *Kaunsaa Buaa* sitting at our house. She used to be seen there not for any love or affection for our mother or us, but for making and expressing love towards her paramour, who was seen standing lecherously at the platform of his compound of huts. The lad had pockmarks on entire of his face; he was not at all a stuff worth loving, least of all by a buxom and beautiful young lady as *Kaunsaa Buaa* was. I overheard the same *Buaa* several times declaring contemptuously before my mother that the lady Prime Minister of India was a *'Randee'* (prostitute). I felt it queer for she herself was a *'Randee'* by that token, and at the moment as well she was busy gesticulating to her seducer only. How a *Randee* could call another one a *Randee*? She was calling the lady Prime Minister a prostitute because she had married a *Paarasee* boy through the impulse of love, the same love affair, the same slimy act that *Kaunsaa Buaa* was indulged in. Just two episodes! Those were not the only exclusive two accounts of titillating episodes, those were however getting enacted in my immediate vicinity.

I must fast forward the tale to its denouement adding simply that after a year or so the elder brother of *Kaunsaa Buaa* who was in defence forces found out a worthy defence personnel and solemnised her sister's marriage. During that entire ceremony, watching it intently from the stand point of a child, a teenager, I was wondering all along what a fraud it was that was being perpetrated on the life of an innocent lad of defence forces, even as, I was watching the bridegroom in a very happy and gay mood throughout the ceremony and celebrations. He might be surmising, I thought, that he was getting a virgin bride, more so, because she was the sister of his friend, another defence personnel. What a foundation of life-long partnership! *Ab initio* based on the falsehood, deceit and insincerity!

XXX

Table of Contents

16. Manly shame

Enter protagonist

Nature has created man and woman for one another, it can be understood. Nevertheless, that's not the only combination which involves sexual activity. Man and man can also indulge in slimy actions as regards sex.

In this class only, one day when we reached school, we found that an adult from a nearby village, *Mumrejpur,* was present there and he was pleading to our teachers for persuading his grandson, who was our classmate and in our Section only, to continue his studies in the school. The boy, who was a suave and gentle guy, was insisting on not coming to school anymore as the fellow students coming from his village chided him by pronouncing that he had been 'fucked', that is, seduced by an elder boy from the same village. The elder boy who had allegedly fucked him studied in a higher class in our school, and the boy was in our class – seventh standard. I immediately connected the episode with my own shattering episode; the elder boys tend to mindlessly defile the younger lads. The unsuspecting guardians might have given the young boy in custody of the elder boy for taking to school, and as is the natural phenomenon, the elder boy instead of protecting the innocent chap, himself damaged him, enjoying his sexual organs. I found this tendency rampant everywhere thereafter in life.

The young boy was feeling shame, a social shame, and justifiably so. It was not easy to face such libels. I was lucky that my seduction had not been exposed to anyone and it was only a psychic shock for me alone, not a matter of social shame. I took pity on the little boy, of my age only. Do the elders have no other tendency but to defile the youngers lads? I wondered.

The teachers of the school were trying to console the wailing grandfather of the boy, and at the same time, persuading the boy to be sensible and making him to believe that his tormentors were telling a lie, i.e. spreading a canard. Finally, he could be persuaded to continue with his studies. Our PT teacher was very sensible person in such matters; he played a very positive role in resolving this sensitive as well as psychological issue. He asked the boy to play badminton in the playground with none other than me, for I was the star boy of the school and, in the idea of our sensible teacher, by playing with me – such a star - the boy might feel a sense of worth and a boost to his self-esteem. Queerly, though I obeyed the commands of the teacher, I was not amused. I felt that by playing with a boy who had been defamed as having been 'fucked' by an elder boy, I would also be termed as a 'defiled' boy. How crazy! Instead of sympathising with a human being of my age and one who had suffered the same misfortune as I, falling prey to child abuser, I was intending to hate him. Today, I pay homage to my PT teacher who was more sensible than I was!

Nevertheless, the problem of sexual misdeeds was not limited only to young ladies or the young boys or the students only. I felt as if everywhere it was being done. In our village, one primary school teacher, *Sonpaal*, was in that bad habit. He had been seen flirting with the young daughter of our poor neighbour of lower caste and class, and I was myself a witness to his misdeeds, being the immediate neighbour of that poor family. Not only this, he tried to rape the young wife of a *nyaaee* (the family barber) of our village. It so happened that a marriage party had come to our village and the entire village was busy handling the marriage ceremony. Even the male members of the *nyaaee's* family were busy with the marriage ceremony, as they were dutybound to help in respect of menial chores of the marriage.

Sonpaal, a rogue and dissipated young fellow as he was, was looking for such opportunity only. He approached the *kutcha* house of the young menial lower caste person and tried to seduce the beautiful young wife of his. She raised an alarm however, and the word spread like wild fire in the entire village. Then *Sonpaal* saved his prestige by resorting to lies; he pleaded that he regarded the young lady as his daughter. Rascal par excellence! Everybody in the village knew that *Sonpaal* was that sort of a bad character, and that he was telling a lie in denying his overtures, yet nobody could gather courage to do anything!

I felt deeply hurt nonetheless. The young boy whose wife was eve- teased thus was none other than the wife of my close friend in fact. I was expecting in the wake of this incident that the village elders would thrash *Sonpaal* and teach him a lesson, and that the *nyaaees* would thrash him; nonetheless, nothing of the sort happened. Nobody could teach a lesson to a bully and a strongman, particularly, if one was also a wealthy person, and a bad

character. *Sonpaal* was a *noveu riche,* a teacher in a primary school, born of low breed, and a rogue; who could tackle him! At least in Indian society! Indian society is good only for punishing gentle guys and soft offenders, not the big offenders, mafiosi and dreaded criminals. The latter rather assume the status of political leaders.

XXX

Table of Contents

17. Mumrejpur *Teacher Manhandled*

Enter protagonist

When I resumed my studies in *Inaayatpur* school after returning from my *Nanihaal* out of compulsions created by the sickness of my father, I came across a bizarre news making rounds there in that one of our teachers, that is, the one hailing from *Mumrejpur* village had been 'beaten' by a rogue person, a bully, hailing from another nearby village. This bully was a notorious person called *Veer Naaraayan*; he hailed from the village *'Kapanaa'* which was situated beside the banks of a canal called *'Gangaa Nahar',* the same water channel that we had to cross quite often while coming from our village to school.

On hearing this news, bad news, I felt shocked. Thus far, for me, the teacher was a sacrosanct entity who couldn't be disrespected, couldn't be mistreated by anybody.

That any Tom, Dick and Harry could savagely mistreat even a teacher was blasphemous and outrageous act for me the child on the part of the offender. I enquired of my elder cousin: "What was the causative factor for this maltreatment, this outrageous treatment of our teacher?"

In fact, on receiving this news I had also derived a perverse pleasure in my heart, the reason being that though he had done me no harm, he seemed to be somewhat arrogant, a conceited person which he certainly was not, even as, in fact he was a dynamic and energetic person. The reason was that he had his younger brother in our class and that boy was somewhat jealous towards me – as was quite natural in the scheme of things of this Creation -- seeing my first position in the class, and also, due to my popularity amongst the pretty lasses of my class as well as school, which was none of my fault though. He could never beat me in academic terms; I was always on top. But this factor vitiated my behaviour pattern not only against the classmate, but also, against his elder brother, the teacher in question. In a sense, I was pleased that the teacher had been manhandled by a bully. In fact that bully was well-known to my father, and he was the elder brother of one of the boys who had manhandled the PT teacher at the town school, in the aftermath of

which, my father had been eased off from the *ad hoc* job he held thereat. The same group of boys had sought admission in this village school of ours after their ouster when it started functioning here two to three years back courtesy of the benevolent lady *Kelaa Buaa* as we called her venerably.

And, for this group of rascals had tasted blood – the blood of beating the teachers – here also it so happened that the teacher in question one day tried to discipline the rowdy boys by using harsh words, and also, slapping them softly on their cheeks. That teacherly treatment was nevertheless unacceptable to the vulgar guys, an utterly spoilt band of urchins as they were. They felt humiliated, unbeknown to the fact that the beatings at the hands of a teacher were a blessing, a boon, as was propounded those days by the wily teachers who were fond of flogging the gullible guys. The boys reached their village and the first job they did after reaching their hamlet was to complain to *Veer Naaraayan* about the objectionable incident – of their beatings at the hands of the teacher. It was totally unacceptable to their patron, the elder brother, the bully, for it was exactly the same act of a teacher at town school that had resulted in their expulsion from the town's school in the wake of manhandling of the PT teacher. Of course, at the instigation and support from my brainless father! *Veer Naaraayan* solaced the weeping boys and assured them that they would be avenged sooner than later. He enquired about the whereabouts of the teacher and the path the latter usually took while going to school.

He observed the path of the teacher for some time hiding in the bushes beside the dust way. One day, when the teacher was all alone and hurrying off towards the school from his village in the morning, *Veer Naaraayan* pounded out of the bushes of wattles from the sideways and accosted the gentle teacher. He didn't feel a need to cross check the information given him by his band of urchins. He caught hold of the teacher grabbing the latter by the collar and slapped in the face on both the cheeks unrepentantly. So shameful! The poor teacher felt embarrassed as well as non-plussed. He could not make out anything of the outrageous action of the bully. He, of course, was familiar with the person and his misdemeanours and notoriety.

When the teacher asked him about the cause of that treatment the rascal barked back by saying: "How dare you touch our boys? Mind your actions in future!"

Humiliation is always a demoralising affair, and that too, of a teacher, that too, in front of the students of the same school in which he pursued the job of teaching.

Disgusted, disheartened, huffing and puffing, he reached the school and narrated the whole gory affair to the teachers and the management whatsoever it was at the school. But to no avail. As I said earlier, nobody in India can take on a bully, a mafia, a big offender, a murderer and a politician. All the punishments are restricted to merely the gentle guys who happen to commit petty crimes and who can inflict no harm on administrative and judicial authorities! Nobody had the courage to take action against the notorious rogue. Nor did anybody report the matter to police, albeit the latter were all the more rascals; they would have terrorised the victim instead, for they were hands in glove with the mafia already.

The incident went into oblivion as everything goes with the passage of time. We passed the classes and reached higher classes after one or two years. One day we heard on reaching the school that *Sonpaal* – the same vulgar and lecherous youth, the primary teacher – had beaten *Veer Naaraayan* and in the school itself. It so happened that teachers community of both Primary and Higher Secondary schools devised a plot against *Veer Naaraayan*; they invited the latter to the school feigning to be organising a function in honour of the bully on some fake pretext. The mindless bully took the bait and reached the school well-dressed and in a happy mood. When the function was going on and *Veer Naaraayan* was utterly gay and happy, in high spirits, *Sonpaal* arose from his seat and reached him, and without any warning or provocation, slapped him in the face, on both the cheeks, and also, simultaneously abusing the bully in worst possible slang involving fucking of the vaginas of mothers and sisters of the bully.

That was shocking for everybody present there, for nobody had suspected such a daredevil act on the part of *Sonpaal*. Not only this, *Sonpaal* challenged *Veer Naaraayan* if he could take on him while passing by our village. In fact the village of *Veer Naraayan* was linked to ours by the dust way and *Veer Naaraayan* had to take the dust way to the town frequently, and the residences of *Sonpaal* and his clan, chiefly of male members, were on the side-lines of the same dust-way. How could *Veer Naraayan* take on a bully of the same proportions as he was!

On hearing the latter news in fact we children were shocked for we feared that *Veer Naaraayan* was a bigger bully in comparison to *Sonpaal*; however, it was not true. *Sonpaal* was better placed geographically, and his clansmen were equally uncultured, savage and lacking every streak of self-esteem, the essential traits for becoming a mafia don, bully or a goon.

XXX
Table of Contents

18. *Father Departs To* Ajmer

Enter protagonist

Father was sick, inflicted with the disease related to sexual organ. At one time it seemed to be fatal. Thanks the rustic treatment of a kind-hearted *Muslim* quack, his treatment by way of using *Matthaa* (the butter milk) saved the life of my father. That a *Muslim* had shown kindness towards a dying *Hindoo* was another mystery for me at that age. By that time I thought that *Hindoos* and *Muslims* were meant to do harm only to one another. However, that was not the truth; they were equally placed and helped each other as a human being should help another human being. Simply by donning the different garbs one does not become a different species; one always remains a human being only.

The academic session had already begun. My father had been eased off from the *Veerpuraa* school as well, for what reason, can only be guessed. One, he was sexually sick; secondly, he had embezzled Rs.200/- from the school fees collected by him, from the Head Master of the school, to be precise, for recovery of which, the Head master and his wife who belonged to our village only kept on frequenting our house – the refugee house, of course – for many years, for almost a decade. In the millet field where I and my father were engaged in removing the weeds in the sultry season, he had told me the entire tale of this two hundred rupees. When I enquired of him why the gentle lady had to visit our home and our father so many times, and why it was so that my father had not repaid her hundred rupees (one hundred he had already repaid, when and how, I do not know), my father had responded with a distorted face and with warped brows howling, "I did not repay deliberately!"

That became all the more mysterious for me. Why a person like my father, who claimed himself to be a righteous person, and also, whom the entire common folks of the village and the small area considered as an honest man, should have opted to not repay the money borrowed from someone, that too, from the Head Master of one's school. Not only this, from the honourable relatives of the same village! However, my father did not offer any plausible reason for adopting such an unrighteous stance, except that I was obliged to draw the conclusion that his approach was starkly *adhaammik* (unethical).

And no misdeed or *adharma* goes unpunished in the scheme of things of the mysterious – or not so mysterious – Creation, the vast Nature!

My father took to fatal disease involving the genitals. Somehow he was spared of untimely death; for his own good deeds or for the good luck of his issues, nobody can vouchsafe. Even his having survived the obscene disease was of no worldly use for the issues and family. He was a non-entity and despite his being alive we felt like being orphans throughout our lives.

There were no means of livelihood. Mere scanty agricultural produce that was harvested normally could not foot the bill of the pretty large household. How my mother managed the household expenses those days was none of my concern; I was under the impression that it was the duty of every pair of parents to manage the financial affairs of their family deftly and capably. Also, I thought those days that every parent was capable of arranging the necessaries of living for their progenies. Nevertheless, this was true only in converse sense, in the absence of this faculty. My parents were a glaring example of incapable parents who could not afford even two morsels of foodgrains for their issues and family; an entity which was incidentally their own creation, rather a fallout of their foolishness.

Leave apart the concerns of earning a living, even life itself of the father was doubtful. However, our patrons, the uncle and aunt who had given us refuge in their abandoned house only took pity on the indolent couple. They visited the village on purpose this time round, the purpose of taking my father to *Ajmer* for treatment of latter's sexual disease. There, they had a Govt doctor of our caste – a double bonanza – and an acquaintance of our uncle and aunt, a fast as well as family friend. A doctor is a doctor, my uncle and aunt thought. They had the impression that once a doctor, one could cure every disease whatsoever. However, that was not true; a doctor could cure only a few type of sicknesses, not all, only those ones for which the doctor had been trained. Still, for my parents had no wherewithal to take any sort of treatment, except the *Matthaa* therapy from quacks, they took my father to *Ajmer*.

I felt so glad thinking that now my father would be cured surely and certainly; I had so much faith in the capabilities of doctors! More so, in the goodwill of our benefactors! Also, I felt a great amount of gratitude towards my uncle and aunt musing that relationships and humanity were so intact still. Nothing was true; they had taken this step merely to assuage the feelings of relatives who had been cajoling them to help our parents, the wretches, the moneyless apes.

How fickle are the relations can be gauged from the fact that our real uncle and aunt – that is, the elder brother of my father – did not venture to help him at all, neither money-wise, nor sympathy-wise. There was no question of my grandfather helping, even as, the latter was absolutely worthless, in a literal sense. He did not have a penny, nor did he involve himself in the financial affairs of the family, he had never in his life, having assigned the entire burden to his elder son, that is, my father's elder brother. Thus even the relations were sham, having no substance in reality, I realised it, palpably.

That my father had gone away was a matter of extreme relief for us kids for yet another reason as well, that is, because he was such a fastidious fellow, a querulous guy, always creating ruckus in the house. His presence itself in the household was a cause enough to create an eruption of volcano of negativity in the family. We the kids heaved a sigh of deep relief contemplating that our querulous father would there be no more at the village, and that there onward our mother and all of us could live peacefully and in tranquillity. At least peacefully! As regards livelihood, he was as good as not being alive. The entire burden was on our gentle and sensible mother.

Another reason why I was glad was that I thought that having gone to *Ajmer*, now my father would get a job. I was under the childish impression that in cities, in urban environs, it was highly likely that one would get a job, and getting a teaching job was certainly easier. If not a permanent or Govt job, I thought, the tuitions were a surety at towns and urban centres. It might be true, however, all such assumptions were applicable to only industrious and diligent creatures, not the senseless, deranged and indolent array of species my father belonged to!

At this juncture, after so many decades of this incident, I suppose, he had returned from *Ajmer* within two months only, without either having been cured of his shameful disease, or having got any prospect of earning a living. He had such a long life before him! Not only his own life, but also, the lives of three kids and his wife! On his return, we were shocked, for, one, he would again start creating mayhem in the serene household, second, he had lost the opportunity to gain any employment. It was the year 1969, and he was hardly 35 then. The service-worthy age was supposed to be up to 60 years even those days. I therefore always felt traumatised by the thought that my father's age was passing without gathering any moss, and I wondered what would happen to us and to him if his entire age was wasted in that manner. Also that how he would live his life without earning anything! This thought crossed my mind, for I saw all around, that the fathers of all other boys and girls of my age were earning and saving money for their future and

exigencies; nothing of the sort was happening all around us. Here was my father who did not have even foodgrains to feed us; he had to borrow that stuff also, that too, in piecemeal! Rather, everything was moribund in our household, everything was degenerating, including lives themselves. At that time, my parents had only three issues: me and my two younger sisters. However, the same year, after nine months, they begot my younger brother, to my utter surprise and dismay. I wondered how they could have conceived an issue with a diseased genital, for my father's illness was concerning the procreational organ only.

Why my father returned so desperately from *Ajmer*? The mystery was solved in the millet field only. I asked my father why he returned from *Ajmer* without trying his luck at tuitions or teaching job there. He spurned the question by saying that his brother and sister-in-law were not sincere in his treatment, also, in his getting an avenue of earning there.

"Why? They had themselves taken you along!"

"That was all for showing off! Only to show to people that they were helpful and broad-hearted!"

"Which they really were not!" I sighed.

Nevertheless, the mystery was resolved sometime later when

my uncle and his eldest son visited our village in the harvest season. On a cursory enquiry by one of the villagers about why my father had not stayed at *Ajmer*, they clarified that he felt scandalised by the remarks of the Doctor *Saahab* who commented that the sort of disease my father was inflicted with were inflicted on the people who had connections with the prostitutes or tramps. To the query why he had not been retained there for taking at least the tuitions, they clarified utterly contemptuously, rather, derisively, "He knows nothing about English; he is a sham teacher. He has conned certain sentences of English and keeps on teaching those only to the students…. For instance, he invariably asks the students to translate the sentence: स्टेशन पहुँचने से पहले गाड़ी छूट गयी थी। (The train had left before I reached the station)" etc.

"His train did always depart before he reached the station.", they further added with added emphasis on derision.

Both the revelations were heart-shattering for me, the child, and also, to the well-wisher uncle who had raised the issue in good faith. My father was an escapist beyond any iota of doubt.

XXX

Table of Contents

19. Gaandhee's Centenary: My Tryst With His Truth!
Enter protagonist

In the entire episode, I am not dwelling on the areas beyond my paternal household, I have an impression of. Life does not flow merely around our own homestead or refugee home; it flows all around alike the winds in the firmament. There was my *Naanee's* household at not-so-far a distance in the same district of the province. However, it felt quite a distance at that time!

In the year 1969, the marriage of the daughter of our younger maternal uncle was solemnised. In the same year fell the *Gaandhee's* centenary: on 2nd of October, 1969. On the occasion of the Centenary, all sorts of functions were organised by the Govt or, more truly, by the governing dynasty. The governing dynasty of *Nehroos* were deeply obligated to this hypocrite fellow whose surname they had borrowed and had added to theirs for deriving political mileage therefrom. They were astute enough to think that it was *Gaandhee's* name that could be encashed politically, not the one of 'Nehroos'. The fabricated popularity that this man had been accorded was propagated by the new regime by neglecting the contributions and sacrifices of the thousands and lakhs of heroes of the freedom struggle over a century or so. Therefore, it was the entire Govt machinery that was engaged in glorifying a sham saint, a crony *Mahaatmaa*. For their own good, for advancing their own political and dynastic destiny! To the detriment of country, that is, *Bhaarat!*

Gaandhee was a very shrewd and cunning politician: he was not a saint, a holy man in reality, and he knew it well. He was actually picked up by the erstwhile wily lawyers of the country as a brainless mascot for rallying the brainless masses behind him for furthering their own selfish political ambitions, i.e.; for grabbing power to govern and rule, and for dislodging the then dominating ruling clan – the princely states and *zamindaars* and *nawaabs*), yet he feigned to be a *'mahaatmaa'*.

He was an autocrat, a dictator in every practical sense, even as, he seldom regarded and honoured the wisdom and wise counsel of common man, except for fooling them around behind him; he overturned majority decisions e.g.; in the case of *Subhaash* as INC president, and in the case of *Sardaar Patel* as preferred PM choice of *Bhaarat*, yet he feigned to be a 'democrat'. Nothing can be farther from the truth.

He was an anarchist in every literal sense, even as, he taught and led people to break the rule of law; and that anarchic habit, that anarchy has now become an accepted norm in post-colonial India for incendiaries and secessionists. Yet he disguised this anarchic misdeed of his proclaiming it as 'civil disobedience', albeit it was patently an uncivil and vulgar act.

He lacked common sense even in normal eventualities, which resulted in untold miseries in the form of displacement and rape of womenfolk for both *Hindoos* and *Muslims* during the sinful act of 'partition' for the multitudes of innocent and unsuspecting countrymen, yet he prided in being dubbed as 'Father of the Nation'. The bitter reality is that even his own issues didn't consider him their 'father' or, at least, worthy of being called as such.

He claimed himself to be an adorer of Truth, yet he deliberately and astutely grabbed whole credit greedily and meanly for himself alone, for getting the transfer of power from Britishers to *Nehroos alias* cloned *Gaandhees*), whilst, in fact, it was a voluntary decision of Britishers to quit India, who were victorious in WWII, however, petrified and horrified by the military might of INA, and at the same time, incredulous of the loyalty of, rather, suspicious of likely revolt by the Indian armed forces.

Only vote-based politics of the present day India is supportive of the survival of *Gaandhee's* fake phenomenon in annals, that too, only for the time being; yet in public esteem and psyche at large, *Gaandhee* and his fake cloned dynasty is nothing short of a sore point for the country, and a hateful entity that represents everything intriguing in the Nation's present day memory.

In the long term, or at the earliest opportunity possible, the country would like to seek 'good riddance' of *Gaandhee*'s supercilious phenomenon! And it will resurrect the true heroes of the nation, *Subhaash* and *Sardaar Patel*, the former the 'Victor of Freedom', and the latter the 'Builder of the Nation', the Iron Men, both!

People are blind *bhaktas* of *Gaandhee* without even knowing his real character. *Gaandhee* showed his true fangs to *Ambedkar*. *Gaandhee* was anti-*Ambedkar*; *Ambedkar* was a *de facto* deity – however never deified. *Gaandhee* was a fabricated saint – an undeserving *'Mahaatmaa'*!

People hate his killer, *Godse,* however ignorantly, i.e. without even knowing the *'G'* of his real persona... that is, the real character behind this much maligned name.

But this is India! Where anything spurious can be sold for 'real'; and anything real can be defamed as being 'unreal', 'spurious' or 'untouchable....!' etc.

Gaandhee was blank about the contemporary social milieu and realities. He should not have meddled with the political system in that case.

During the partition of August 1947, *Gaandhee* was deeply pained. He had lost faith in all his close aides. When he came to know of the news of *Hindoos* and *Muslims* slaughtering each other, he refused to believe it. To get a first-hand account, he sent *Pt Chaturvedee* to *Laahaur*. Upon reaching the city, the *Pandit* saw that it was the *Hindoos* who were being tortured and killed in the area. He himself was attacked, stabbed several times, and buried neck deep in a sand pit but was thankfully saved by an army officer. When he narrated the situation to *Gaandheejee*, the *Mahaatmaa* refused to believe him, saying that the *Pandit* was prejudiced because he was a *Hindoo* himself. *Pt Chaturvedee* was deeply hurt that *Gaandheejee* had lost faith in him. Upset, he returned to *Bangalore*. Three days later, on 30 January 1948, *Gaandhee* was assassinated.

Gaandhee got what he deserved -- his violent end -- not because he was not a *Mahaatmaa* or because he had any ill-will towards anybody, but because, he made millions of innocent countrymen -- of all faiths: *Muslims, Sikhs, Hindoos*, all our compatriots -- suffer in utter agony of what they call partition: the rapes, displacements, massacres, mayhem, and as an aftermath, a never ending atmosphere or chain of terrorism due to his sheer lack of the knack of social pulse, the lack of social knowledge. He did not have even the simple common sense that partition would lead to mayhem, rapes, massacres and displacements, which even a standard one student would have had a prescience of. The judgement of history is given on the ground, i.e. based on the fallouts of a politician's actions, not merely on the basis of his hollow and ill-conceived intentions!

One solid proof of this conviction is that Providence meted out to him a violent end commensurate with his cold insensitivity towards lakhs of innocent sufferers of partition who would definitely have cursed him from the bottoms of their hearts while being looted, raped, murdered, displaced from their ancestral as well as century-old habitats, and their physical existences being mutilated *et al.*

Simply being politically correct is not being morally sound as well, necessarily. Truthfulness warrants courage to uncover a corpse and show the bloody side of its reality, *Mahaatmaa* or no *Mahaatmaa*!

Gaandhee's prevailing image is based on the crutches or patronage of Govt., not on the public perception. Public perception of *Gaandhee*, particularly, of the youth, is entirely at odds with whatever is tried to be projected through Govt machinery out of compulsions of political expediency.

Gaandhee's failing is that he lacked that insight, i.e.; the capability to foresee all those degenerative developments post 'Freedom'!

Freedom has virtually assumed the connotation of *en bloc* 'Freedom from Ethical Living and Thinking!'

To blame only *Gaandhee* is not fair, some sympathisers argue. They also argue that the most ambitious *Mohd Jinnaah* was the person who is responsible for partition, and that the farsightedness, or so to say, the political expediency and selfishness of some leaders also compelled *Gaandhee* to accept partition. They argue if one could imagine a democratic India with *Paakistaan* and *Baangladesh,* then east *Paakistaan*, being parts of it? In that eventuality, India would have another *Moghul* state for next one thousand or so years eliminating the clan of *Hindoos*. The state of *Kashmeeree Pandits* would have been that of all *Hindoos*. The only thing *Gaandhee* can be held responsible for is his pro-*muslim* stance, they aver.

To such people, I have the argument that whereas I appreciate what they share out of adoration for *Gaandhee*, I do not dispute that, but my only sore point is the rapes, the displacements, the dismemberments, the murders, the massacres, the genocides *et al* of millions of *Hindoos* and *Muslims*, as well. What was their fault? They were living in their sweet homes at their birthplaces unaware of nefarious designs of political buffoons, be it, arguably, *Jinnaah* (for *Hindoos*), or *Jawaahar* or *Gaandhee* (for *Muslims*). The latter had only their individual interests in mind, not of those millions who suffered in the name of '*Aazaadee*'. It had no meaning for those, none of them calls these venerable names, *Gaandhee, Jawaahar* or *Jinnaah*, with respect; they call them all sorts of names, rather.

Only those who did not suffer the pangs of partition and were safe in their dens are insensitive towards those who suffered all those unspeakable agonies.

If even after creation of a *Muslim* land, rather, two, *Paak* and *Baanglaa*, the problem —the supremacy of *muslims* -- is persisting as they say, like in *Kashmeer*, it shows the uselessness of the remedy adopted. The formula, as the history has vindicated, has failed.

Even now, there is no guarantee that India will not become a *Moghul* state, given the state of polity in India.

Division or no division, no political leader has a moral right to subject the unassuming millions to such fatal fate, simply for satiating one's appetite for fame –*Gaandhee* -- and throne –*Jawaahar* -- and country --*Jinnaah*.

Furthermore, if *Hindoos* were so weak, as to be susceptible to being dominated by *Muslims* and India getting converted into a *Moghul* state, they deserved it. No weak species deserves *Aazaadee*, the freedom. The price of freedom is bravery and valour!

Better option in that case would have been to perpetuate the reign of westerners who were strong enough to tackle both *Hindoos* and *Muslims*, both weak and rascals enough, and also, willing to prostrate before the Britishers.

In that case, *Gaandhee* ought not to have meddled with such a sensitive issue as *Aazaadee* from Britishers because that in other words meant subjugating in turn to *Mughals*. I think, *Gaandhee* and his protege themselves had never contemplated or spared a moment to ponder over these matters of crucial importance. And that was their failing!

That's why millions suffered unspeakable miseries as a fallout of what we living in safe dens and having lost no dear ones, dub as *Aazaadee*! And in which, the political class of yesteryears wallowed remorselessly and shamelessly.

The 'J' duo --*Jawaahar* & *Jinnaah* -- cut the baby (Post-colonial India) down in the middle!

Gaandhee and his protégé had never imagined in their farthest or wildest dreams that they would ever get freedom from Britishers; that is why they never felt it necessary or even worthwhile to contemplate over the ticklish issue of how to grab/ snatch power from *Moghuls* who were holding forte till 1857, and transfer it to *Hindoos*. They had taken it as a given that Freedom from Britain meant power for *Hindoos* since democratic rule implied majoritarian rule, that is, rule of *Hindoos*, by virtue of their majority in the country.

Ironically, when this arguably undeserved, or uncalled for, wild dream, so to say, suddenly materialized or came true, that too, immaturely, that is, before time, unexpectedly, paradoxically as a bolt from the blue, they were caught unawares, unprepared totally for holding it. That reminds me of the great feats of *Shiva* in the wake of the emergence of poison from the process of churning of oceans; at that juncture, it was he only who could handle that momentous calamity. Or, likewise, at the time of descent of the great river *Gangaa,* from the mythological heaven, whose tumultuous torrents at that crucial moment of transition only *Shiva* could control. There was none of that stature at the time of tumultuous transfer of power from whites to blacks who could control the currents of ethnic violence by locking them within one's hair-locks! They found themselves faced with the genie of erstwhile *Moghuls* staking claim to the throne, figuratively, *Duryodhana* staking claim to the throne whereas the *Paandavas* being the heirs apparent to the erstwhile ruling king, *Paandu,* thought that they were naturally entitled to the throne of *Hastinaapur,* whereas *Duryodhana*

didn't think so. *Jinnaah* didn't think so, even so!

Gaandhee and his protege could take on civilized and law-abiding Britishers owing to the formers' nuisance value but found themselves unequal to or, so to say, no match for *Moghuls/ Muslims* who did not believe in any such concept as the civilized or the law-bound behaviour. For the Britishers, the law had primacy, whilst for *Moghuls*, the brute force was everything to justify the entitlement to throne.

The brains of *Gaandhee* and his accomplices of freedom movement were not so sharp or strong as to find a non-violent solution to this grave situation, so to say, to handle this, figuratively put, sword which was double-edged. No logic could deny *Moghuls* their right to the throne if Britishers were to leave, since former were the rulers of India till 1857.

So, instead of proving their logic or strength or force against the *Moghuls,* the 'J' duo - *Jawaahar* and *Jinnaah* - connived to share the exploits of the freedom movement between themselves, proverbially, cutting the baby down in the middle, and both being foolishly happy and satisfied that both of them had got their share of the baby, whereas none had. How foolish! The baby was no more: 'freedom' was dead on the spot, at birth itself. Still, there was lot of merry-making – merriment --

on both the sides of the recently erected fence within the vast country on the pretext of a new baby's birth. Eunuchs were dancing as though as they do on the birth of a baby!

And there could be heard heart-wrenching cries in the background, those of millions of countrymen who were being displaced, looted, dispossessed, raped, deprived, dismembered, massacred *et al.*

Moreover, how can the countrymen respect a person of dual character? *Gaandhee* was reportedly in support of hanging of *Sardaar Bhagat Singh, Raajguru* and *Sukhdev* on the argument of *Ahimsaa;* nonetheless, he wasn't only in opposition of punishment to *Abdul Rashid*, the killer of *Swaamee Shardhaanand*, but also, was in support of his action i.e. the killing of the venerable *Swaamee Jee* by saying that *Swaamee Jee* was preaching *'Ghar Vaapasee'*, known as *'Shuddhi Karan'*.

Many may argue that there might be things which could be done in different ways, however, nobody is God here, and also, that *Gaandheejee* is the one who united the Indians together by bracing up their self-respect.

We, who were born with silver spoon of freedom in our mouths, perhaps never could understand the sacrifices of the freedom fighters, and could seldom feel the agony and shame of reading the bill-boards forewarning 'Dogs and Indians are not allowed'. A country or a society can never sustain by betraying those who fought for them.

Who knows we might stamp him as a traitor in the coming days; fingers are crossed.

What one is saying against *Gaandhee* is all imaginary and hypothetical, one might argue, and that some of *Gaandhee*'s decisions, if those had been taken in a different way, might look better to us these days. It is always arguable. But given the circumstances obtaining at that time, those were perhaps the better options if not the best. Taking hard decisions demands guts and is ever a difficult task; it is hardest when it involves fates of others as well. Nevertheless, this fallacy cannot disqualify him for commanding respect from his fellow countrymen - then and now. He is the one who united the Indians across the land; his sacrifices and contributions cannot be forgotten nevertheless. Who will praise our heroes when we, their countrymen, do not? Some might aver. Some might also say that they are not in the league of those who decry *Gaandhee*, and are rather proud of him. Someone even argued in his support that *Gaandhee* contributed a lot to the propagation of *Hindee.*

To such people, my argument is that their sphere of knowledge is limited, and also, inchoate! I am not saying that he did not know *Hindee*. That was his *mazbooree,* for no politician can afford not to know *Hindee* and become a national leader in this land.

I am saying, rather, that he and *Nehroo* were the stooges of Britishers and got the reins of Governance from the latter, not because Britishers were forced by the former out, but because it was conducive for the Britishers to hand over the reins to their stooges so that they could negate the prestige and achievements of *Subhaash* -- who was the real victor of Freedom movement -- and they could manage to evacuate themselves from here safely, which was not possible if the transfer had been through the INA. .....

Nevertheless, the reality of history like a subterranean serpent slithers out with the passage of time, however, one might try to camouflage or hide it otherwise.

Gaandhee was the stooge of Britishers; he was acting on the lines/ advice/ caveat of Mountbatten who had put the pre-condition before *Gaandhee* that the Britishers would hand over the reins of India to only and only *Nehroo,* who was a lesser Indian/ non-Indian, and rather, more of an Englishman and as good as a Britisher only! Britishers felt it expedient to hand over the reins of their colony to their stooges, first, for undermining the gains/ invincibility of the INA or *Subhaash*, and secondly, for ensuring their safe exit/ safe passage while fleeing from here, lest they should have been butchered by the valiant warriors of INA and the common folks in their wake! The Englishmen had had this bitter experience in 1857, when their children and women had been butchered by the so-called revolutionaries, heinously and dastardly although.

Exactly that was the sour memory of the past why *Gaandhee* was coerced/ pressurised by Mountbatten, in turn, at the behest of Britain, to manoeuvre the political moves so as to make their conducive stooge as the new ruler of India. And that's the testimony of *Gaandhee's* democratic credentials! Even when *Nehroo* was sworn in as the PM of India, the Governor General was Mountbatten himself only, whither Freedom!

Gaandhee was a hypocrite in essence, not at all a worshipper of truth: he felt, psychiatrically, alike a psychopath, that he followed the path of truth, but in fact he was a hypocrite whereby despite following falsehood he showed off as an experimenter of truth! And gullible common folks adore him for as they say, जो जीता वही सिकंदर' , that is, nothing succeeds like success, and one who grabs the throne first, grabs it in perpetuity, for ever! And that's what's happening in India!

The British thinking behind

the Partition was that the Partition was not the natural corollary of *Hindoo-Muslim* or, for that matter, the *Sikh* incompatibility, rather, it was the well thought out political expediency on the part of Britishers who had witnessed the valour of Indian armed forces during World War II; rather, they had won the war owing to the valour of Indian soldiers only.

So far as this phenomenon is concerned, the same applies to *Muslim* rulers who ruled here for almost a millennium; they won the wars because, on behalf of them those who were fighting and dying on both sides were none other than the Indian natives only! Fools only!

Britishers got to realise quite vividly that Indian Army – such a strong/ formidable force – if that were allowed to remain intact, in its the then obtaining state, would prove to be lethal for any army whosoever throughout the world; and Britain being the world leader by that time could not afford to overlook that supremacy of anybody, not to speak of Indians who had been under their subjugation owing to the latter's foolishness/ gullibility. They, therefore, thought it expedient to instigate the largest ethnic group in India – the *Muslims* – to demand an unthinkable entity – a separate nation - in the name of religion/ communalism; and also, when the latter raised the demand, they promptly accepted and got

acquiesced, as already premeditated.

That stratagem has served them and the world well thereafter, for ever. Since the Partition, the Indian Army – that was – has been fighting among themselves only falsely camouflaging themselves as the Indian, the *Paakistaanee* or the *Baanglaadeshee* armies, or lately, the guerrillas/ the terrorists of *Jammoo* and *Kashmeer*!

That's the testimony to the wisdom of those who claim themselves to have gained Independence! At the cost of Partition! For two men's welfare only: *Nehroo* and *Jinnaah!*

XXX

Table of Contents

20. *My Trip To* Aleegarh *And* Gaandhee Jayantee

Enter protagonist

Despite all my harangue in the foregoing paragraphs against the arguably the most venerable political personality throughout the world, let me rush to claim that my father was a staunch fan and supporter of *Gaandheejee*. He was badly brainwashed by the propaganda machinery of the Govt of the time. He loved to read the literature and books on *Gaandhee* and was wont to eulogise *Gaandhee* during the gossips and chats with the folks in the village and also in the trains or buses with the co-passengers. Nonetheless, with the passage of time when the misdeeds of partition started oozing out at the seams of the bandages administered by the erstwhile Govt my father had a shock of life when the young generation started upbraiding him for praising a hypocrite, an unworthy person claiming oneself to be the 'Father of the Nation'.

Having come across no other true version of the tale of Partition, and that of the murder of *Gaandhee* in the wake of annihilation as well as mutilation of tens of millions of people who had no say in deciding the fate of their country, I was also blindly faithful to the *Mahaatmaa*'s publicised as well as fabricated image. During that duration – of celebrations of Centenary -- I happened to be in my *Nanihaal* in connection with the marriage of the daughter of my younger maternal uncle. When the marriage ceremony was over and the guests had started departing after long stays of rest and merriment in our *Nanihaal, Surendradaa* decided to visit *Aleegarh*, his place of stay for studies with his father, my *Maamaajee*. I had never been to that often proclaimed Elysium of *Surendradaa* and other elders, that is, the town of *Aleegarh*.

During the marriage mayhem or merriment, I had observed, and *Surendradaa* made no effort to hide it, too, that he had affair of romance with a pretty girl of his own age who had come to attend the marriage ceremony and who resided in the same neighbourhood at *Aleegarh*. The girl was often seen during the hustle-bustle of marriage ceremony gesticulating and beckoning to *Surendradaa* standing on the roofs of the big mansion type buildings of our *Nanihaal*, and it could be noticed by whosoever willed to see them. *Surendradaa* was such an attractive and sensuous personality for adolescent lasses at that age, and even thereafter, when he was a grown up adult. Some people are the incarnations of *Pradyumna*, the progeny of Lord *Krishna*, who is supposed to be the incarnation of *Kaam Dev* himself, as is delineated in the mythological texts. *Pradyumna* certainly did not attain *Nirvaana*, and might have been born as *Surendradaa*, no gainsaying the fact; and that girl might have been the incarnation of *Raadhaa*, who knows? The cycle of life and death has been continuing unbroken like that, and no living being knows anything about one's earlier births as well as roles played by them at erstwhile places of birth!

This was not an exclusive or single incident when *Surendradaa* was seen indulging freely and openly in affairs concerning fair sex; he was seen doing such things with so many other pretty girls including those at the small hamlet itself. There was at the hamlet an exotically beauteous damsel of almost his age and her name was *Raaj Kumaaree*. Not only by physique, she was seductive by way of countenance as well with slender lips, singular frame etc. *Daadaa* was extremely enamoured of her beauty, and she also didn't mind *Daadaa's* overtures towards her. *Daadaa* was often seen sighing seductively on seeing her and also commenting lecherously: 'Oh, how lucky would be the one who would wed her and sleep with her!' We the kids of lesser endowments as regards beauty and fortune felt a shudder on hearing such outright outrageous remarks of *Daadaa*. And the girl kept on gaining age and flesh on her carnal body. One day I could see *Daadaa* flirting with her in my presence in the fields of maize during a rainy season when it was drizzling and the weather was salubrious and seductive, too. However, in my foolishness, when I made some endearing remarks towards the pretty girl, instead of getting pleased and lured, she rebuked me and warned me, even threatening that she would disclose my impropriety to my mother and other elders of my maternal relatives in that village. I didn't have the spine to proceed further, and thus withdrew myself. But I wondered why she did not objected to *Daadaa* doing the same thing, that is, from showing advances in the same manner towards her.

Once however she got angry with *Daadaa* and complained to her father and her father, though a poor person of the village and of a *Braahman* cast, tried to take up the issue with *Daadaa* but could not, for our *maamaajee* intervened and proffered the logic as to what the girl was doing in the field where *Daadaa* was, and also, that the girl had no business to visit our fields where she had no job at all. A poor person cannot take on a wealthy and well-to-do person even if one's daughter is fucked or befouled.

Daadaa did not mind even doing the same foul acts with the male adolescents even.

I fancied during that tenure that I should also accompany *Surendradaa* to *Aleegarh*, even as, I fancied to be friends on equal terms with that attractive personality, *Surendradaa*. And my mother agreed to my proposal. We set off on a childish sojourn towards the 'city'. When we were on way to the railway station, while nearing the primary school where I had studied during my fifth standard, we stumbled upon a Ten Rupee note lying on the dust path. *Daadaa* noticed it and jumped with joy on finding it. Since the guests of marriage party were departing those days quite in large numbers, it was a no brainer that the note had been lost by some guest of ours. His loss was our gain, however. We were very happy; it was a good omen for our journey to the city! Ten Rupee by the standards of those days was quite a hefty sum, it need be kept in mind.

However, *daadaa* pocketed it and I merely drew virtual pleasure thinking that I was an equal partner in the spoils of the new-found riches.

On reaching *Aleegarh,* where we were alone and on our own as children, we enjoyed loitering around freely in the streets of the neighbourhood. Also, I came across a school magazine lying at the rented quarters which was totally devoted to the *Mahaatmaa's* centenary. I pounced upon the magazine forthwith as a hungry person would on seeing the food, and felt as if I had found a treasure trove. I esteemed the *Mahaatmaa* very highly, and finding study material on his life was nothing short of a miracle for me. However, now in hindsight, I feel that whatever all was published there in that magazine was mere rhetorical and mere eulogizing of a not-so-worthy person, of a person who had been a lynchpin in destroying the lives and chastity of tens of millions of poor and common folks of undivided India.

During the sojourn to *Aleegarh,* I got however disillusioned as regards my equation with *Surendradaa.* However friendly and on equal terms I considered myself vis-à-vis *daada,* he did not consider me worthy of his friendship or equal to him. He considered me a petty wretch, the son of a resourceless father only. A larger chunk of my

zeal that was generated in the wake of our journey to the city for the first time, that too, all alone, was gone. I felt that *daadaa's* behaviour at his urban residence was starkly at variance with his behaviour at village. At city centre he was behaving somewhat like a stranger with me, as a superior personage. Thus, I could have a feel of lack of intimacy and lack of warmth in relations in the hearts of urbanite people.

I continued to harbour the foolish hope that out of the money that had been showered on us by Providence in the shape of a Ten Rupee note, *daadaa* would share with me five rupees, half the gain. When he did not venture to do this at *Aleegarh,* I thought he would do this judicious correction of equi-distribution of spoils after returning to the village. We returned to the village after two days but *daadaa* did not share his bounty with me, even as, he broadcasted the news in the entire village that he had found a Ten Rupee note lying on the way. All the guests had left by that time and nobody came back to claim one's lost money.

XXX

Table of Contents

21. Towards The Yogaasans

Enter protagonist

My grandfather and father both had a good collection of books, books of both *Hindee* and English.

My father having a spiritual inclination had books concerning spirituality and mythology as well, whereas the books collected by my grandfather were those of the era of Britishers; the latter was a student of the B R College, *Aagaraa*. Education being a scarce commodity those days when my grandfather tried to get educated, we were proud of our grandfather, and we used to pronounce the name of the college with a sense of pride and superiority as *'Rao Balwant Singh* College, *Aagaraa'*. *Rao* was the king of *Awaagadh* and was of our clan, also, distantly related to our relatives and family. He himself being an illiterate person, is reported to have established the college for the issues of *kshatriya* clan, for they were mostly unlettered, and as a fallout utterly uncivilized and vulgar.

As I was sharp at studies, and also, fond of reading the written word, I was always on the lookout for books. Books seemed to me like lovely lasses, very precious and very enjoyable. I was not interested in lasses at all nonetheless. One day when my father was away at *Ajmer* in connection with treatment of his sexual disease, I happened to rummage through his stock of books. And amongst them I stumbled upon, *inter alia,* a book entitled *'Yogaasan'* by *Vitthal Daas Modee* of *Aarogya Mandir* repute. Given there in the book printed entirely on glazed paper

there were portraits of various postures of *Aasans*. I was thrilled to see them. Moreover, there was the book on *Upanishads*; it was a special edition or number of *'Kalyaan'*, the religious magazine entitled *'Upanishad Ank'*. I was mesmerised by both the otherworldly books.

Whereas the *Upanishad Ank* was food for my curiosities about the Creation and the world that always haunted me, the book on *Yogaasans* was a queer thing for me to set off on an adventure quite novel for me. I started reading the book and while going through the content about the benefits of doing *Yogaasans*, I felt extremely inclined to pursue *Yogaasans*. Also, I intuitively felt that it was meant for me only. At times I had observed my father doing some *aasans* but quite rarely as well as irregularly; he seemed to be an expert in pursuing 'irregularity' *per se.*

During the reading of this book only I realised that *Yoga* is not only *Yogaasans* but an entire regimen of disciplines involving eight aspects, viz; *Yama, Niyama, Aasan, Praanaayaam, Pratyaahaar, Dhaaranaa, Dhyaan* and *Samaadhi.* Then I became all the more enthused to pursue all the eight aspects of *Yoga* instead of getting overawed or discouraged. That coupled with *Upanishads* made a rich cocktail for me to launch myself on the heady journey of spirituality and attainment of *Moksha*, the *Nirvaan*. I realised in definite terms that life was not meant merely going to school and playing the games, rather, it entailed lot many sublime things that I had to attain if I intended to live really a life.

I started with *Sheershaasan* which was mentioned as the first and foremost *aasan* in the beginning of the book. Nevertheless, it seemed to be the toughest one. But I decided to go gradually with mastering every single posture of the *Aasan* slowly and slowly, and thereafter only to proceed to the next posture. And this expediency worked. Within a fortnight I was standing on my head with legs pointing towards the sky. Then there was the *vardhit sheershaasan*, which involved bending of the spinal cord etc and I mastered that as well within no time. I was under the impression that by doing *Sheershasan* I attained something miraculously abnormal, some sort of a *Siddhi*.

And indeed I had! The *Yogaasans* that I was doing improved not only my health but also the mental calibre beyond my expectations and imagination. That was palpably apparent to me. But like everything has its flip side, this aspect had its flip side too. Since the *Yogaasans* started affording a divine hue to my countenance, to the already handsome and attractive one, the menace of pretty and enchanting girls that I was facing already at my school became all the more intensive and terrible. Alongside, my resolve not to fall in their clutches also kept on becoming stronger and stronger. I did not hate those girls but I felt extremely annoyed at their overtures and wished they were not there in my class.

School course and curriculum for me became like a kid's game, of which, I was a connoisseur. My performance in the exams in which I was already on top became all the more shiny.

I mastered almost all the postures of *Aasans* given in the book and practised them daily and zealously. During the winter season it was such a pleasure to do all the *Yogaasans* in the small courtyard of my refugee home!

XXX

Table of Contents

22. Yogmudraa *and Experience Of Nothingness, i.e. Absolute Void*
Enter protagonist

This was such a fortunate patch of life at my village, even as, we were staying in the house of our elder uncle, the husband of my mother's elder sister! I could undertake the *Yogaasans* without any hindrance whatsoever from the side of family members. Nonetheless, the *yogaasans* had engendered in my mind a sense of exclusivity instead of broadening it in that I always thought that no other person should now practise *Yogaasans,* as though that was my exclusive preserve. That was placing me in an exclusive and exotic club in the entire area. Coupled with the superb performance that I was giving in the school, this pursuit of *Yogaasans* added a unique hue to my aura.

I am saying that my heart developed a meanness as regards others adopting the practice of *Yogaasanas* and *Praanaayaams*; that is based on empirical data in that in our neighbourhood a younger son of one of my uncles of the village also started doing *Yogaasans,* and when I came to know of this development I set off feeling jealous. When he himself and his elders pleaded with me to guide and assist the young boy in this respect, I hesitated and ultimately did not guide him. I thought that if I helped him, he would be equal to me in *Yogaasans* and that I would lose my exclusivity. So mean indeed I was, now I realise! But childhood is like that only. Instead of broadening my heart and mind, the *Yogaasans* were being used by me as a means to aggravate the ill-will, conceit and arrogance, which were quite contrary to the objective of *Yoga*.

Based on the instructions provided in the book of my father, I kept on treading the path of *Yogaasans* covering one by one almost all the postures. And I felt elevated day by day. Those days I practised *'Yog-Mudraa'* as well. This was the posture wherein after sitting in lotus posture I bent my back forward making my head to touch the navel, with the result that the entire body assumed the shape almost of a ball. The respiration in that posture became very much restricted and did enter every nook and corner of the body. Not only this, in that posture I could contemplate super naturally, I felt.

One day, when I was in the posture of *'Yog-Mudraa'* I started pondering over the outermost limits of things and phenomena obtaining in the universe. I started with my body which was at that time in the posture of a ball. Beyond my body there was the house whose walls were the outer limit for that thing. But beyond the house there was the village whose outer limits were known, too. By that analogy, there must be the outer limits of the district, the state and the country and these were there in fact. Eventually, the planet Earth, too, has a limit, with its definite size and shape. However, that was not the end of the things available for the contemplation of my consciousness. There were astral things, like, the moon, the sun, the stars, the planets, and beyond them, too, the constellations, not one or two, innumerable ones. I presumed eventually that all those thinkable entities could be encircled in my imagination within a broader sphere, navigating on an outer periphery of that all massive stuff.

However, what was beyond that? I thought. This question sprung up from my heart no sooner than I had reached that outer limit of the broader sphere, within which are supposed to be ensconced all those humongously sizeable and mind-bogglingly colossus entities. I thought, based, on my surmises, that there might be innumerable such world systems in the unknown universe; let all those world systems and constellations be encircled together, *en bloc,* in a mammoth sphere, and keep on enlarging the sphere's size as well as volume so as to encompass everything whatsoever could have been omitted from being ensconced inside it. Then I assumed that whatever material or constructs were there anywhere throughout the tangible or intangible world systems all had been incorporated inside a super-duper sphere.

Nevertheless, beyond that? This question posed itself before me like an apparition, a spectre, again, as soon as I finished drawing the supposedly largest sphere of my consciousness. Beyond that is also supposed to be anything there, and that is definitely present there. Somewhere! Not somewhere, here itself! I am part and parcel of that broadest mystery, the largest sphere of the inexpressibility. Plausible answer might be: 'Nothing'! But that 'nothing' itself is a crucial thing, for that's there, a void. In the terms of cosmic proportions this 'Nothing' becomes the most tangible and the most pervading phenomenon. Supposing that a 'void' is there, a 'nothing', a 'naught', I drew a still larger, rather, yet another largest sphere so as to incorporate even that void and also all such voids inside it. That went and still goes beyond the pale of my thinking power and even the broadest imagination. Suppose there is nothing beyond that! And this supposition becomes the most ludicrous supposition, for obviously there is something, however, called 'nothing' or whatever, not even nothing, so to say.

Still, the biggest mystery is that there is the question: then what is beyond that, there, if nothing is there. At least 'nothing' is there! This nothingness is the most intractable mystery of the universe.

In the process of going on enlarging the size of such spheres to more and more broader spheres, I ultimately reached a point – the outer limit of my consciousness – where I felt that there is nothing, even this nothing is not there.

Then what is all this? That which seems to be so real, so meaningful, so crucial to tackle and deal with in our lives, during our living process? For which the creatures are at the necks of one another! Sheer foolishness! Isn't it?

There is nothing anywhere.

Absolute void! This revelation ought to have filled my heart with a sense of enlightenment, but I got utterly frightened instead. Badly terrified. In the unbearable glare of this absolute truth of the Creation I sought refuge in the falsity of notions of the conscious world. That was much more relieving to heart, mind and consciousness. I abandoned the further journey and aborted the *Yog-Mudraa*, too, forthwith.

Nevertheless, later on, when I realised that the same was a great realisation at the level of *Pragyaa*, and that I should have continued with the investigation of the truth, I tried to pursue the same experience again, but I could not. I could never repeat that real experience. It was once in a lifetime experience nonetheless! Thereafter, I have never been able to experience that absolute reality.

Nonetheless, that realisation has dented my worldly demeanour; I feel like I am playing some fake play, feeling fully conscious that whatever I am doing, seemingly howsoever crucial or important in mundane terms, is but meaningless and immaterial only. Ultimately, there is nothing to be kept or preserved for good. Ultimately, nothing matters here. Everything and everybody will vanish in the future, even as, everything and everybody has vanished in the past.

After that experience, I tried to describe that experience in words and in diary and by talking to my peer level friends, and even to my supposedly seasoned father, but to no avail; nobody could get a clue to what I meant to convey. For them, only the known world was the outer limit of the life and the life's concerns!

Later on, in my life, when I came across the tale of *Gaargee* and *Yaagyavalkya,* and later on the tale of *Upgupt* and *Vaasavdattaa* in the *Buddha*'s tales, I noticed that the same phenomenon was discerned, rather, their interactions did end at the same point. *Yaagyavalkya* forbade *Gaargee* from asking questions beyond the *'Brahma',* even so, *Upgupt* restricted *Vaasavdatta* from asking questions on *'Nibbaan'*. I derived utmost pleasure from those tales of enlightened ones thinking that perhaps those questions were the figments of our imagination, or might be those were the products of our consciousness only, there being nothing as such what we think through our consciousness as the entities, the phenomena, the world or the world systems.

XXX

Table of Contents

23. My Two Year Old Sister Falls Sick

Enter protagonist

Ushaa, the beauteous girl of two or so, whom I liked so much due to her sprightly demeanour and divine beauty, and felt proud for her being my younger sister. She was such an asset; beauty is always an asset! In all the ages! When our father was away once at his school at *Veerpuraa*, she had fallen sick having stomach-ache. First my mother administered various rural medicines, herbs etc as remedies for relieving the pain on the advice of elderly ladies of the neighbourhood, but the little pretty girl did not feel any relief and cried and kept on crying incessantly.

After a day or two, my mother could not bear it and decided to show her to the quack doctors at *Jhaajhar*. But the problem with the people inhabiting these rural and rustic environs is that they are totally backward; they do not permit their ladies to venture out even if they are faced with dilemmas involving impending death. My mother could not go to the town as a fallout of this tradition. Then what to do? We did not have any vehicle either, the bullock cart or a *rehloo*. Now how to take a two year old child to the town and consult the doctor?

Faced with this intractable problem, my mother finally decided to depute me to carry the little sister to the town accompanied by my younger sister of seven. I agreed enthusiastically, since I thought I could carry the load of my two or so years old sister easily, for I had been carrying her in my lap in the village for making her play outside along with the other kids. But playing in the village with kids for a few minutes or half an hour is one thing whereas carrying the child for two and a half kilometres, that too, a sick child whose entire weight multiplies due to sickness, is just another thing.

I and my sister took our youngest sister gladly to the town, and also, the baby felt well while going to a town, but on the return journey, out of exhaustion or what – I don't know -- she started crying. She was actually finding her stomach-ache, rather, pneumonia, aggravated as I myself being a child was not carrying her properly and she was feeling constant pain in her abdomen. On return journey I got tired and started jerking my sister in exasperation. My another sister of seven who was accompanying me was in a dilemma as to what to do; she wanted to help me but she could neither carry the youngest sister, the baby, nor could she help me in any other manner. She was merely trying to solace the baby and me. At that time I was so frustrated that I forgot all the relations. I felt that it was only one's physical comforts that mattered, nothing else in this life. In the eventuality of one's body and mind being put to inconvenience and discomfort, one forgot every relationship whatsoever.

After much struggling and facing utter dejection, when we were still quite far from the village, in came one of the villagers, an elderly uncle of ours, *Doongar,* who was otherwise a regular boozer, but at that moment he was in good senses. When he saw the little girl in pain and me and my younger sister in equal distress, he offered to help us. He could handle the baby in a more conducive manner. On reaching a comfortable position and pose the baby became silent. Also, the elderly person was kind-hearted; he had chosen to help us out of humanly kindness and compassion only. He was talking to the baby in childlike manner and the baby became silent out of curiosity being on the lap of a stranger. We both – my younger sister and I -- also felt extreme relief in that moment of utter frustration. In our hearts, we blessed the elderly man and thanked the humanity. A human being ought to help another creature in distress!

On reaching home, we narrated the whole tale of woes to our mother and also complained against the innocent little baby's recalcitrance, being entirely oblivious of the fact that the baby was innocent and was in real pain. My mother showed sympathy with all the three of us. At the material time, there appeared on the scene one of our neighbours, a kindly grandee, and he did some domestic trick, sort of remedy and the child felt some relief.

But I set on the train of thinking that I was living in a hugely savage society which lacked common sense and which restricted the liberty of half or more proportion of the society to their own disadvantage, and in the process, people like us were suffering untellably, as we did.

And the fathers, the begetters of babes, those like ours were utterly unconcerned. They were merely concerned about their own individual comforts: their bodies, clothes and sham prestige.

XXX

Table of Contents

24. Birth Of A Brother And Calamitous Portents

Enter protagonist

Even as my father was unemployed during the year when I was in standard seventh, I had little clue as to how my mother was managing the expenses of the household. Father was not taking even the tuitions at that age as he did in the later years. The time would have been quite taxing for my mother, no doubt.

In that year only, my younger brother was born on the intervening night of *Deepaawalee* and *Govardhan Pooja.* In fact I was not aware by the day of his birth that my mother was pregnant, that is, carrying a child inside her womb; I was so innocent!

We had celebrated *Deepaawalee* the evening before and

had gone to sleep. What sort of *Deepaawalee* it would have been can be gauged from the fact that my father being an unemployed there was abject poverty in the family. We had somehow managed to buy half a kg *Kheels (*puffed rice), the puffed rice and hardly an array of fire crackers purchased for a pittance that had been managed, in turn, by selling the old rough copies and some old yet precious books. Whatever money was acquired by selling the supposedly worthless parchments was made to correspond to the requirements of the shopping for the *Deepaawalee.*

Nevertheless, this penury and wretchedness was no peculiarity for us; we had been having such experiences aplenty in wretchedness all along our small life-spans.

We had no clue as to what was afoot the night ahead, i.e. between *Deepaawalee Poojaa* and *Govardhan Poojaa*; we the three kids, me and my two younger sisters. Our parents would have been fully aware though. At around midnight, we noticed some disturbance in our refugee house; our father was rushing towards the midwife – *Kallaa* – who had been the traditional family midwife for generations, even as, her predecessors had been to the previous generations of our kinsmen. *Kallaa* was in fact residing beside our residences only, on the rear side of our *Khedaa*. She could be called from

our *Khedaa*, too. She was a seasoned nurse and an utterly pragmatic lady, though hailing from the so-called lower caste. Our *Chhote daadaa* was often seen calling *Kallaa* from his *Chaupaal,* that is, the other end of our *Khedaa* on which our male residences were perched on the other side. *Daadaa* was equally pragmatic; though he was very rude, he was not rustic; he was fond of studying the religious texts, like *Satyaarth Prakaash* of *Swaamee Dayaanand* and other *Aarya Samaaj* literature, apart from the study of *Panchaang*. By virtue of his being conversant with and fond of *Panchaang*, he was virtually a *Pandit* for the village folks for deciding and declaring the dates for celebrating various *Hindoo* festivals.

My father thus rushed to call *Kallaa*, however, not from our side of *Khedaa* but going to her house treading the dust way leading to her hut in the small and claustrophobic area inhabited by poor lower caste people, the poor strata of our society.

Before heading towards *Kallaa* for hailing her, my father had called the neighbouring girl, the daughter of our neighbourer, our aunt, named *Mahaaraanee*. In that house, there were so many *Raanees*, the queens! My mother seemed to have already made arrangement with *Mahaaraanee buaa* about this eventuality, for after confinement to the nursing room, that is, the room where her child was to be begotten, someone, preferably a lady was required to take care of the household, so as to cook the food etc and to take care of the small kids, already three there. I was 12 at that time, my younger sisters were 7 and 2, respectively.

After queerly piercing and bewailing cries of our mother for some time, it was declared that a boy had been born in our abode. On the mid-point of *Deepaawalee* and *Govardhan*! My parents and us three kids too felt it good ominous to have got a new addition to the population of household on the occasion of the festival of wealth, the *Lakshmee*. Since we were poor, we were always on the lookout for good omens. However, nothing of the sort happened in the immediate living conditions, nor in the near or far off future. Rather, the boy turned out to be a destroyer of the family establishment and whatever was there available in the form of wealth, at least the arable land. He sold off the residential areas as well, and ultimately getting bogged down by his indebtedness and the vicious cycle thereof he finally disbanded the establishment at the village, thus shutting the doors on the ancestral village, our native place for good. But this was later on. In the immediate instance nonetheless there was generation of profuse hope and pleasure in the household.

I, however, wondered that so far I was the only son to my parents. This realisation occurred to me that night that then onward I had a brother. We were now two. So far my parents were ever anxious about my safety and kept on worrying that they had only one son and if anything happened to him, that is, me, what would happen to the propagation of their clan! Meaning thereby, now they won't mind if I died somehow! I felt my importance plummet with immediate effect.

I also wondered that our parents did not have the wherewithal to run the household at all, so far so that they could not manage even the cereals for basic food for the small family. How could they think of increasing the size of the family in those dire circumstances!

I recounted in this connection the night when during February that year my father had visited the village having come from his school at *Veerpuraa*. Outwardly, I had observed that he never behaved amiably with my mother, his wife. During the night nonetheless, when they – my parents – presumed that we the three kids were asleep, sound asleep, they came closer. I was not asleep by that time. I made a move on my cot changing the sides. My father so as to ascertain that I was asleep or not asked softly; 'Are you awake?'

In that awkward situation what else could I have said but

keeping mum. Had I spoken, it would have been quite embarrassing for all of us, rather, the shame for lifelong for both myself and my parents together. I kept mum, however, facing a bizarre dilemma, suspecting the enactment of a drama which no issue is supposed to watch in one's life. When I didn't respond, nor did both of my younger sisters, my parents went ahead with their love making as usual. Normally, there must be nothing unusual about love making, even as, everybody is fully conscious that a woman and a gent meet each other and do sexual intercourse when in isolation. But openly, it is prohibited and rightly so. That duration of about half an hour of my parents' love making was a real torture for me. How could I help avoid it? During that episode of love making I heard my father make such remarks to his wife as were never expected of him in outer world, in the open. In the open world, he was like a daemon and never behaved as a human being. In love making he was so soft! I drew a satisfaction in my heart that in the inner core of his heart my father was also as soft as any other masculine gender. Nonetheless, I was mistaken, for in the very next morning, I saw my father mistreating my gentle mother cruelly and uncivilly as he ever did so far. I related that episode to the birth of my younger brother.

During her role as the caretaker of our household, *Mahaaraanee buaajee* was quite soft in demeanour towards us kids and behaved just like a close relative or our blood relation. During those ten or so days of our mother's confinement to the nursing room, we felt as though she was our own aunt, though she belonged to some other household, not our own. We were small kids and lacked the faculty of differentiating between human beings on the basis of 'mine' or 'yours' or 'theirs'. However, our mother did not think so. Instead of feeling grateful to the gentle and helpful aunt, the first thing she asked us kids on resuming her duties as a normal housewife was: 'Did *Mahaaraanee* rummage through any of our boxes or anything else?'

I felt shocked at this meanness of my mother's heart. I used to take my mother to be a lady of higher norms and having a broader mind and heart so far. I felt disappointed; the truth was not like that. As soon as her requirement was over, he threw the aunt like a fly in the sweet dish and did not feel any gratitude towards the girl. She instead gifted her a cheap saree and felt as if the service the latter had offered had been compensated by way of that cheap saree. Ingratitude is the gravest sin a human being can do, I realised; and going by the fate my mother has been stalked with I now feel vindicated.

My younger brother's various *sanskaars* and variegated functions were organised by my father with lot of enthusiasm and fanfare, calling *Panditjee* of repute from the town. That much credibility the scions of this family still retained in the area in that the persons of repute obliged them to visit personally. *Panditjee* prophesied that the boy was a very lucky boy and that he would increase the fame of the family all around.

In the spirit and enthusiasm of having got another son, my father was prompt to rebuke me many times during the solemnisation of these functions and rituals; and I started feeling disheartened as well as discarded.

Those were the days of winter and our father was unemployed; and we were passing through a very pathetic patch in time. My mother had begotten a baby boy but did not have proper food to feed herself and the new-born. Therefore, she and the child both were irritated and felt annoyance at slightest excuses.

One day when we were enjoying sunshine outside our refuge home, our new baby was sleeping on a small *Peedhaa* (small cot of 2'x2') in the coy sunshine in front of the door inside the four walls of the not so impressive refuge. I was studying my course books as usual sitting outside the door and my father was whiling away time, doing nothing as usual, as was his wont.

Suddenly, we heard the pounding of the hoofs of a mare; yes, it was a mare running unbridled in the cattle ground in front of our house. The master, the owner of the mare, our near relative only – a cousin – was chasing the mare desperately, huffing and puffing in the chase. But how could a human match the speed of a young mare! After making two or three rounds of the vast cattle ground, the mare headed towards our small door. In fact, the stable of the mare was almost alike our refuge. The poor cattle could not make out whether this was her stable or the house of wretched human beings unlike hers. When my father saw the mare approach the door, his eyes got wide open in exasperation. On the other hand, when our *Mahaaraanee buaajee* saw this unprecedented spectacle unfolding before her eyes, she rushed to the spot where the baby was sleeping and lapping it up rushed inside the room. Nevertheless, the mare did not stop, she entered the room, in which she could hardly fit herself well; the room was so tiny as well as claustrophobic by the standpoint of a beast. It was good for only wretches like us, not for equestrian beasts. The quick witted aunt clambered up the small niche, or the window, so to say, inside the room. It was not far from the mouth or rear legs of the beast. Had the mare opted, she could have dismantled the entire room and its walls by kicking briskly around. However, she did not chose to go berserk.

We missed our heart-beats. We were face to face with death, imminent death, having entered in the physical form of an equestrian death in our house or refuge. So death was still chasing us!

I thought in my fancies that my father would be angry with the person whose mare it was, but he didn't. He was brave only before his wife and poor children. Faced with the outsiders and strong men he played a perfect coward. He did not even express his resentment or annoyance to the men, his nephew.

The hind legs of the mare were in the door of the room. Now, how to enter the room and catch the mare by the bridle, was a crucial question. And without entering the room, it was not possible to bridle the mare and take it out. However, the sporty man was an expert of handling the horses and mares. Somehow he entered the room escaping the likely fatal kicks of the mare, and caught it by neck. The stoutly shaped mare was gentle, I think, or it was befuddled not to see her own known environs in that narrow space, so that it obeyed every command of her master and came out of the house.

We heaved a sigh of relief; all of us, including the master of the mare.

Thus was our house of refuge defiled by the scent of the beast for ever. Now nobody could claim that we were not staying in a stable.

We thanked God, and also, we appreciated the quick wit of our aunt to have jumped to the conclusion that the mare would enter the interior room and lapped the baby in the nick of the hour and ahead of the mare -- hardly one yard ahead – hastened to clamber up the window, which itself was hardly enough to accommodate her.

XXX

Table of Contents

25. Pandit *Boy Thrashes Me Unprovoked Before The Guests, My Cousins*

Enter protagonist

Like every year in the season of summer our benefactors, that is, our *Mausee* and *Mausaajee* happened to visit the village, and for we were staying in their house only, they stayed there only. Along with them came the entire entourage of their large family: 8 children and the couple themselves. Though a burdensome prospect from the standpoint of our father's financial condition, it was a special festive season for us children. Throughout the year, the academic year, we kept on exerting through the dreary terrain of dry academics and text books and there was not much indulgence with the village folks. The arrival of so many of our cousins was a sort of boon for us. And we felt proud, too, on getting this unbidden wealth of relationships. Also, during this one month's period, there were made special arrangements for exotic foods and fruits: rustic ice candies, water melons, musk melons, mangoes etc. How can I forget the soirees to *Bambaa* – the water brook -- that flowed near our village! In which we swam unmindful of the dirty quality of water and the risks involved in the manner of snake bites. We were forewarned and sounded by the elders that there lived a snake beneath or in the vicinity of the bridge where we took bath in the brook.

Nevertheless, the seemingly demographic boon was not without its flip side. Some of the boys of our age even turned jealous towards us and tried to show their superiority in front of our guests, the cousins. Some even became vulgar to the intolerable extent. For instance, one *Naypaal*, threatened one of our cousins without any provocation that he would set the latter right. Such episodes soured the mirthful atmosphere, however, but could not be helped. Those episodes resembled the barking of dogs or getting bitten by them while going on the road silently and without troubling the dog.

Yet another such incident took place during one evening when we were all playing in a field near our village. We were enjoying it, myself included. I was so gay and happy at that moment! At that moment, a boy of the village, the son of a *Braahman*, who was returning from his fields from beyond our fields, and who was as well a classmate of mine, happened to pass by along with his father and uncle. I felt doubly gay to see him, even as, I thought, he would help me spruce up my image in front of my guests.

Instead, he pounced upon me as a wild wolf as soon as he reached our playground, that is, the ploughed field where we were making merry. I was totally unprepared, however. He started wrestling with me without any warning, his father witnessing the vulgarity of his son. Probably his father only had instigated his son to thrash me down and make me lick the dust so as to show his prowess before our relatives or guests, so to say. The village culture was and is like that only. I felt suffocated with this sudden onslaught of an urchin whom I supposed to be my well-wisher. I found myself physically weaker than this guy. Maybe it was due to our diets. He was the son of a farmer who could afford milk and healthy foods to his progeny whereas I was the son of a father who could not even manage two morsels of food to fill the belly. How could then I take on a rural boy on equal terms!

Nonetheless, I got a shock of life. In the process, I felt, I could even die due to suffocation, lack of breath, for I was feeling short of breath during that unprovoked onslaught by an urchin.

I also felt foolishly that since my cousins were ours, they would come to my rescue, but none of them did, and advisably so, now I feel, for that could have had cascading effect of flaring up the rift between the two parties which were otherwise indulged in only a mirthful wrestling feat. Then I realised that nobody was anybody's relative in this universe, especially, in the human world, and also, that nobody came to anybody's rescue when faced with danger to one's own life; also that everybody saved one's own skin in such eventualities. One must trust only one's own calibre and strength.

However, we did not narrate this embarrassing as well as humiliating episode to anybody at our home. This sort of anarchy was quite common in the rural milieu we lived in. It was not even worth mentioning. Still, I felt, the import of this incident was not less than that of the episode of *Mahuaa* tree and the throwing of scythe by the insensible farmer scaping my life by only a few yards. Back then I had been saved by the skin of my teeth from the sure-shot death. I mused whether death was still playing hide and seek with me? Was the death on the prowl

around me in various garbs and kept on attacking me unprovoked.

The one month of summer passed fleetingly and the entire entertaining entourage departed finally. The amount of pleasure that we gained at the time of their arrival came to naught and we felt extremely sad at the time of their departure. But life is like that only. At that time they merely departed from the village for returning the next year, but as of today, they are nowhere, most of them having departed from the known world – the visible world -- for good, having vanished from the arena of existence on Earth. That is yet another and a much bigger mystery as well as misery!

XXX

Table of Contents

26. Visit Of VIP Guest From Somnaa and My Neglectful Attitude Towards Him

Enter protagonist

During that summer only there did visit our family one of our relatives, a VIP one in local parlance, that is, the erstwhile *Zameendaar* of *Somnaa;* the same personage under whose awe the in-laws of our maternal uncle's son had accorded me very high regard during the latter's *Gaunaa* ceremony when I had been to their village as mentioned hereinbefore. With the abolition of *Zamindaaree* system by the new dispensation post transfer of power from Britishers to *Nehroos*, the financial conditions of each one of them had deteriorated miserably, pathetically, to be precise. They were, nevertheless, not rich or well-to-do in the previous dispensation for any special acumen or giftedness of theirs, rather, they were privileged and pampered ones, favoured by the erstwhile regimen, to the disadvantage of poor people whom the former dubbed as 'inferior castes', or down-trodden ones, which later on became 'scheduled castes' and 'scheduled tribes'.

For a while post abolition and usurpation of his *zameendaaree,* however, the headman of the family at *Somnaa* was accorded the same amount of respect and veneration as he was getting during his hey-days, and in consideration thereof, he was appointed as a member on the management committees of various schools and educational institutions including the one at *Veerpuraa* village where my father had served. But gradually, when the common folks came to realise that there was nothing awful or abnormal about the stature or calibre of those persons, they started neglecting them, even as, their financial conditions started betraying their wretchedness in various forms and on multiple occasions. The grand man was actually the husband of my grandfather's elder sister. He was a very respected person at one time;

also, the *Buaa* of my father, the wife of old man, was very high-flying lady, full of utter arrogance and conceit as is expected of such pampered ladies hailing from ancestrally well-to-do households.

Times had changed somehow and with the advancement of his age the grand old man started feeling the pangs of neglect and, in turn, fell prey to the ailment of depression. In such a melancholy mood, he deserted his home and came for a short trip to his relatives at ours. In fact, in the past, he had seen the same family in its best splendour. Nonetheless, owing to the same phenomenon by which his own lot had suffered drastic downfall, our financial condition was all the more miserable; my father was not able to afford even the two morsels of food for his not-so-small family. The old man found the scenario of our village and especially our households quite in contrast to what he had expected in his mind.

Not only the physique of the living creatures keeps on undergoing astonishingly unrecognisable changes over the time, even the shapes and forms of non-living things and phenomena keep on changing continuously over the time, even including the financial conditions and the feelings of relatives, depending upon their respective states of mind and physique.

The old man felt crest-fallen and depressed as he already was in; his countenance having assumed a sombre look. He had left his house hoping that he would draw solace at the house of his sometime well-to-do relatives, but here it was all the more pathetic. So far as my father's family was concerned, it was the worst lot of the entire *Badwaalaa* clan. He lacked even food grains. The old man had come to our father's home – not home, rather, refugee hut. He had not been entertained by our elder uncle, with whom the old man had the equal terms of relationship as with our father. Nor did our uncle who had come from *Ajmer* show any special regard and concern for the old man as I noticed, rather, my conceited aunt and following in the footsteps of her elder sister my mother too derided the decrepit and emaciated old man. The only person seen concerned with the old man was my father; and there were reasons behind his concern; he had been obligated to him in terms of the latter having accommodated my father as an *ad hoc* teacher in the school and *Veerpuraa*, and also, having accommodated at his mansion type abode at *Somnaa* for two long years gratuitously, i.e. for free.

During those summer soirees when my cousins were visiting us, I was revelling in the games and plays of variegated hues with them. I was, in the process, not paying any heed to the commands and requirements of those two people, that is, my father and the old man. Yes, I could take notice off and on of those people sitting in a morose mood in the family garden beside the well-head there. Also, our grandfather, whose brother-in-law the old man was meant to be, was seen chatting sitting beside them at various spots in the rustic area. They would be ruing their present fates comparing them with their glorious and conceited pasts. All the three of them! Freedom of India for them implied only this much: perfect devastation of their pelf and prestige! There was nothing worth celebrating for them in the ritual of *Aazaadee.*

Once along with my cousins and other boys I passed by those mirthless people in the garden and my father hailed me abrasively as was his wont and asked me to go unto them and pay my respects to the old man, but I didn't, rather, we all the boys derided them calling them 'worthless old duds', to the consternation of each one of them. However, I was deriving a perverse pleasure by disobeying my father, who in my view did always took company of worthless fellows like himself, like, in this instance again he was sitting with a worthless old fellow whom none else in the family was valuing.

However, I was wondering why my elder uncle who had come

from *Ajmer* was not according any regard for the old man. For, he was not directly related to the old man. It was the trait of those urbanites to respect and honour only those who were directly connected with them. This is the peculiarity of urbanite elites; self-centredness, disgusting selfishness!

Connected with the same episode is the tale of the visit of my father's *Buaajee,* the wife of the great old man. In the prime of youth, the same couple love each other so passionately, and when in advanced age, the same coupe start squabbling piteously as well as grievously; more so, when the fortunes are on the downward slope! Earlier, the husband had fled from the home and took transitory as well as illusory refuge at our refugee camp, but ultimately had to flee when he found the conditions prevailing at his imagined heaven even worse than those at his own home. After a few months of his departure, we found that the lady, his wife, had arrived. Her demeanour and banter betrayed to us effortlessly that he had fled from her house after daring her family members; in simpler terms, telling her family members that if they did not regard her well, she would go to her parental house and live there for good. In fact, the ladies fancy in their stagnant thinking that the same condition would be prevailing at their parental home as

was obtaining during the time when they were adolescent or young, and were meted the best of treatments at the hands of their parents and brothers. They however forget that with the passage of time, in the same way as they themselves had waned, their youth had waned, and their prestige had diminished in their own household, at the other end too where they were fancying to seek refuge everything would have changed: unrecognisably. Not only this, even the lot that loved them would have passed on and an entirely new set of people would be claiming ownership of the property, the household, feelings and relationships there. Nothing of the old set up would be found, so to say!

And exactly, the same thing happened; nobody had time for entertaining the 'poor lady'! Everybody whosoever including my father who was so much obligated to her was busy here in one's own rigmaroles and tantrums of life. For a week or so the people and my father did show regard for the lady, but when they realised that she was in no mood to leave there, they started neglecting her, and at times, not even asking her to have food. My father who was so much obligated to her also started misbehaving with her, to her utter shock and bewilderment. My father was concerned about our education and schooling and he found that the old lady had started making ruckus in our house, as well, exactly on the lines she would have been doing at hers in *Somnaa*, meaning thereby, she used to rebuke my mother etc.

Ultimately, she left after cursing my father and us all. Although we were already a wretched lot, we observed that afterwards we were all the more wretched in financial terms. Maybe the curse of the old lady bore sour fruits for us all: an ungrateful lot!

XXX

Table of Contents

27. School Result And New Summits of Glory

Enter protagonist

When the final result of standard seven in school was declared, my performance was much better, better than what I had expected. I felt even at that juncture that the *Yogaasans* had brought about a paradigm shift in my mental calibre. I could grasp the academic things quite smoothly. I did not exert too much on studies, rather, I used to play a lot and make my body get smeared with dust. My physique felt surcharged and energetic all the time. I derived an indescribable pleasure within my physical frame: all because of *Yogaasans*, I thought. *Yogaasan* was such a panacea for me! Despite my extraneous and playful activities beyond the study table, my performance was impressive and extraordinary. I was on top, that was

a given! I attributed this to the fruits of *Yogaasans*. My father endorsed my views, even as, he seldom practised them; he only rendered lip service as he did in respect of all the other chores of life.

My father was without any source of income that year and had been trying desperately to find one – the only one, that was the *ad hoc* job of English teaching. And the only school that was there was the town school at *Jhaajhar*, from where he had been rusticated two years back. I sometimes wondered why my father did not try his luck at *Inaayatpur*, at my school. However, his version for not doing the teaching job there was that his elder brother, my elder uncle, was a teacher there. I wondered also if it was constitutionally or legally invalid or prohibited to do the teaching job at the same school where one's sibling did the job. However, this was the piece of the figment of imagination of my failed father. He had a bent of mind whereby he sought to seek the logic for failing himself, instead of seeking recourse for succeeding. He was not a success-oriented person.

The same could be said of his father, that is, my grandfather. He was also a failure in his financial life; he had plucked in High School at the B R College, *Aagaraa*, in the beginning of the Century. He did not do any job as well, whereas his friends and classmates rose up to very high and prestigious positions even in the post-Independence era. The result was that he was incapable of helping any of us his grandchildren monetarily. Of course, he was a source of inspiration and a treasure trove of wisdom as well as worldly knowledge but he was useless when it came to supporting us tangibly. His position as a grandfather was of no use or no meaning for us. We had only a notional relationship with him in that sense. We suffered our lots miserably and he was a mere spectator like a stranger. What use such relationship! Even that of a grandfather or a father!

The same genes had passed on to my father. Nonetheless, not to me! I was shining day by day. The entire village eulogized me. Everybody praised me, including the multitudes of pretty girls, both acquainted and unacquainted ones. But I was least interested in 'praise' and 'adulations', also, in 'romance' or affection that I got profusely while passing through any random sphere. I was sort of sick of too much praise; that affected my privacy. I could not enjoy my solitude and privacy. I was taken notice of everywhere, at least that is what I felt in my childish fancies. But that might be true as well, for many a time I found adults beckoning to me and hailing their wards telling them that I was the prodigy who was very brilliant and a gifted one; and I could

over hear their loud voices.

When I visited my *Nanihaal* later on, I boasted of my sterling performance even there and disclosed the secret of that performance by linking it to *Yogaasans* and *Praanaayaams*. With a sense of amazement when my maternal cousins asked me to demonstrate some of the bizarre *Yogic* postures, I enthusiastically started presenting complicated postures of my supple and soft body even in the agricultural fields where we were busy doing the weeding job for the crops. To my aggrandisement and everybody else's amusement and amazement!

However, all this greatness on academic front was no deterrence for my mother from deploying me for chopping the soft dry stems of mustard plants for use as fuel wood in the household. We lacked food as well as fuel wood. I did that chore as well and without any grudge exerting myself even in the scorching sun. Also, my academic and physical performance did not bring about any change in the penury of my father. He lacked wherewithal even to feed us mere food grains as was his wont ever.

I at times wondered why my father was in such dire straits despite his being a sincerely devout person, an honest person and a proclaimed *dhaammik* person of the area. He commanded a lot of respect in the entire cachement area of the village in these aspects. He was in the habit of bringing saints and hermits to our home pretty frequently and getting blessed by serving them. We were also blessed by the saints in the process. But no blessing of the saints could deliver us from the misery of not having even the basic food for filling our bellies. No blessing could bring about upward shift in our financial condition. We remained wretches throughout, at least during the reign or regime of penury of our father.

On thinking about this aspect later on, I realised that it was because my father had been tormenting our mother and us kids constantly, rather, regularly. We kept on cursing him from the bottoms of our hearts, this is also true. And our curses – those of children and ladies – were weightier than the blessings of the saints. This leads to the conclusion that one's actions are more important. It is the actions which bear fruits; mere lip service to *dharma* does not do. Blessings may help but if actions are *adhaammik,* unwholesome, nobody can help one. One's own actions are the only saviours!

XXX

Table of Contents

The End

English Books by *'Videh'*

Hypocrisy & Reality (fiction series: 9 books)

'Hypocrisy & Reality' is a fiction series comprising multiple books – novels. The fiction is aimed at depicting the hypocrisy of human society in every respect, be it the upbringing and treatment of babies, toddlers, children, adolescents, youths, or be it the treatment meted out to adults, aged ones, those who are closely related with oneself, with one's blood; not to speak of those called strangers or outsiders. Barring a rarity, nobody cares two hoots for the sentiments or security and safety of other living creatures on this sole planet nurturing 'living' beings!

Book 1: Beyond the Pale (fiction)

'Beyond the Pale' of Time & Space is the first volume of the long fiction series 'Hypocrisy & Reality' and as the name suggests, it deals with the timespan in the life of the protagonist when one had not even had a tryst with the concepts of Time and Space, nor did they make any difference in one's life if those ubiquitous phenomena were not taken cognizance of. Those were the years before the realm of schooling, the arena of perfect unconcern for the written letters, words, or numbers.

Book 2: Wilderness of Literacy (fiction)

'Wilderness of Literacy' is the second volume in the long fiction series 'Hypocrisy & Reality' and, as the name suggests, it takes the protagonist in the arena of letters, words, and numbers: the realm of what we call the 'literacy'. The experience of a child while treading this seemingly dreaded as well as untrodden landscape is nothing short of venturing into a wilderness; of course, led and mentored first by one's parents and thereafter invariably by their preceptors -- the masters -- all of whom have a tremendous amount of impact on the future human being that emerges from their inputs given and endeavours made towards making a man, the humanity.

Book 3: Advent of Time (fiction)

'Advent of Time' is the third volume in the long fiction series entitled 'Hypocrisy & Reality' and covers the schooling period when the protagonist discovered the phenomenon of Time, and also, figuratively he felt that it was then his time, even as, he mysteriously discovered his latent potential and wisdom catapulting himself into the uppermost orbits of glory, fame and all round applause from his classmates, masters as well as teachers. To his own amazement as well as bewilderment! Nevertheless, this providential blessing was not without its blemishes in the shape of rancour and envy of fellow classmates and their patrons towards him. Even as, Nature never allows anybody pleasure and praise without at the same time associating with them the equivalent amount of pain and back-biting!

Book 4: Devoid of Shelter (fiction)

'Devoid of Shelter', the fourth volume in the long fiction series 'Hypocrisy & Reality' furthers the journey of the protagonist into the world where he discovered to his dismay that he had no place on the globe which he could call as his home; he had no place of his own where he could take shelter during the day, and during the night. He somehow made do with seeking shelter with the relatives – maternal chiefly; not as a transitory phenomenon, but for good, until he himself took command of his life, snatching himself away from the indolent lifestyle of his parents. He also discovered during the refuge that however meritorious one might be, without the good base of ancestry, one was not considered as such.

Book 5: Price of Refuge (fiction)

'Price of Refuge', the fifth volume in the fiction series 'Hypocrisy & Reality' furthers the journey of the protagonist into the world when he returned to his paternal relatives and found to his dismay that his father was absolutely incapable of arranging a dwelling of his own. Also, he found himself to be a mute subject to child abuse at the hands of none other than supposedly an elder cousin of his, the son of his so-called benefactors who provided refuge in their vacant house. That was the price paid by the child for the indolence and handicaps of an unworthy father for seeking shelter under the tutelage of so-called relatives. No refuge seemingly looking innocuous goes without some price to be paid either by self, spouse or one's children.

Book 6: Hatred towards Love (fiction)

'Hatred towards Love', the sixth volume in the fiction series 'Hypocrisy & Reality' furthers the journey of the protagonist into the world where to his amusement he found himself catapulted into the realm of a celebrity or at least a child prodigy as far as the small rural catchment area was concerned. By virtue of his giftedness in the realm of studies and his bewitching countenance, the classmates, especially, the lasses of her age could not help restraining themselves from loving him; and they did it overtly, without caring for the opinions and feelings of other class-fellows. Albeit the protagonist himself wallowed in the faulty ideology that having any truck with fair sex was anathema and a great sin which could not be washed away in later life.

Book 7: Towards the Yoga (fiction)

'Towards the Yoga', the seventh volume in the fiction series 'Hypocrisy & Reality' dwells on the period in the journey of life of the protagonist when he was at the pinnacle of his bodily prowess and psychic acuity, thanks to his habit of pursuing *Yogaasans* regularly as well as religiously. As though something divine was associated with the pursuit of *Yogaasans*, his father luckily could get an *ad hoc* teacher's job in the town school too; however, that was not to be sustained throughout for at the fag-end of the academic session, his father fell out with the Principal of school and was expelled. *Yoga*, nevertheless, gave the protagonist a hue that was unparallelled, and which materialised into the worldly as well as societal fame for him.

Book 8: On the Descent (fiction)

'On the Descent', the eighth volume in the fiction series 'Hypocrisy & Reality' takes the protagonist over the hump. He was then a ward of such a guardian who did not have any wherewithal to run his household, yet had no qualms about begetting more issues, more and more at that. Agriculture, of course, he had as an inheritance but he was by nature averse to anything even distantly associated with agriculture or Nature, for that matter. Any industrious as well as expedient agriculturalist would have eked out one's livelihood quite easily from the fifteen *beeghaa*s of arable land his father had inherited from his resourceful, brave as well as powerful ancestors, but not he.

Book 9: In the Exile (fiction)

'In the Exile', the ninth volume in the fiction series 'Hypocrisy & Reality' furthers the journey of the protagonist into the world where post his dramatic jump into the orbit of fame in the wake of his High School result, he found himself entirely in a barren land where he could see no ray of hope from his father, even as, the latter was totally incapable of arranging the means to further the studies for his exceptionally gifted son. For the first time, the protagonist realised that his father was incapable of meeting his requirements for pursuing further studies. He was already suffering emotionally having been separated from his mother for the first time! This was for him like an exile, that too, very uncomfortable!

Bewailing Muse (poetry)

Be it the sage *Valmeeki* or be it the modern poet *Sumitraa Nandan Pant*, both have held that poetry has its founts in heart and is the outcome of extreme sorrow, misery or pangs of separation. Poetry cannot be created; it gets engendered out of compulsion. From the heart! Heart's language is poetry or musing! I have offered to christen them as Muse: 'Bewailing Muse'; the first musings out of wailings! Nevertheless, I am tempted not to treat them as children's literature for I sense some substantial element, too, in them. The period of the composition of these poems

is from 1972 to 1976; and I feel that my wailings have not fallen on deaf ears, so to say, given my present circumstances of life which are totally opposite to the then prevailing ones!

Chambellion (drama: comedietta)

In the genre of Drama (Comedietta), here is the playlet *'Chambellion'* that exposes the bizarre reality of the political developments post transfer of reins from the whites to the yellow people in the guise of 'Democracy' and 'Independence'; whereas actually the latter have been pursuing their dynastic agenda and propagating their own family fiefdoms that have flourished like weeds in multitudes in the void created by annihilation of Princely states and Landlords. Allegorically, it may be compared with the weed flourishing in an agricultural field which has remained unsown after harvest of the previous crop. For the subjects, verily, there is no Freedom whatsoever, in literal sense.

Brainy Beasts (short stories)

This is an anthology of short stories, included wherein are four short stories or farces, so to say, that is, anecdotes including the 'In An Illegible Script', which is the English version of the author's *Hindee* short story *'Anpadh Lipi Mein...* (अनपढ़ लिपि में)*'* that was first published in now extinct though the then prestigious *Hindee* magazine the *'Kaadambinee'* way back in July, 1992, with quite an applause and accolades from the sides of kind readers! Other stories or anecdotes are also those published in other places, i.e. journals of variegated hues. Nothing uttered in these works is meaningless; this conviction is at work behind the inspiration to publish them in book form for kind readers.

Search for Life (translation of 'Hatyaaree Sadee Mein Jeevan Kee Khoj' (हत्यारी सदी में जीवन की खोज))
English Translation by *'Videh' Arvind Kumar* of *Hindee* poetry book *'Hatyaaree Sadee Mein Jeevan Kee Khoj' (हत्यारी सदी में जीवन की खोज)* by renowned young poet *'Nirvikaar' Mukesh Kumar.* This book has earned *'Nirvikaar'* the award of *'Jai Shankar Prasaad Puraskaar'* of Rs. One Lac from the *'Rajya Karmchaaree Saahitya Sansthaan, Uttar Pradesh'.* On the *Hindee* book *'Hatyaaree Sadee Mein Jeevan Kee Khoj,'* critiques by renowned personalities -- both young and old -- like *Ashwaghosh, Prempaal Sharmaa, Rajeev Saxena, Dr Anoop Singh, Dr Devkee Nandan Sharmaa, Manoj Kumaar Jhaa, Gautam Rajarshi,* etc have been published in various journals and magazines. The renowned critic Dr *Om Nishchal* has included this anthology in the select category for *'Kavya Paridrishya'* of 2017 amongst the famous poetry books.

Reality of Invisible (translation of 'Adrishya Kaa Yathaarth' (अदृश्य का यथार्थ))
English translation by *'Videh' Arvind Kumar* of the *Hindee* poetry book *'Adrishya Kaa Yathaarth' (अदृश्य का यथार्थ)* by renowned poet *'Ashwaghosh' Om Prakaash Sharmaa. 'Ashwaghosh'* -- a well-known moniker of *Hindee*

Procreation, the Adorable (English summary of Shiv Puraan)
The *Shiva-ling* has ever been a matter of

world! A litterateur of impeccable renown! Praised by multitudes -- both in literary and plebeian spheres! He has been composing prolifically -- having published over two dozen books spanning all the genre! The thesis, the short stories, the short epics, the anthologies, the new genre songs, the *ghazals*, the poetry for children *et al.* Covering all age groups! He has been honoured with many awards in literary and academic fields by prestigious institutions.

Nagasaki: Bomb & Aftermath (commentary on the first novel of Nobel Laureate, Kazuo Ishiguro) (Displayed on Oxford bookstore)
This is a work of literary study into the first novel 'The Pale View of Hills' by 2017 Literature Nobel Laureate, Kazuo Ishiguro, who has narrated in a mesmerising style of story telling the tale of Japanese society undergoing change in the aftermath of dropping of atomic bomb. The Americans not only vanquished and occupied the Japanese military and land by dropping the most lethal weapon never before heard of – the atomic bomb – on two of the Japanese cities, one of which was Nagasaki which witnessed this technological devastation on 8th of August, 1945, but also, occupied the minds and hearts of Japanese youth, both men and women. The youth of Japan started decrying everything old and conventional including their erstwhile education system and the ideologies of patriotism and nationalism.

amazement and mystery for mankind. That something obscure is there behind the adoration of such a carnal symbol as *ling* irrespective of the same being that of a deity called *Shiva* has ever been lingering in my mind. Why should a large majority of population in this land – from north to south -- worship the genitals so openly, so brazenly? So reverently! *Shiva* is supposed to be a mythological persona, in existence too long back in time, who might have been the pioneer in realizing the spectacular qualities of *ling* and *yoni,* specifically, those of converting the *sthaavar* (the insensate) into *jangam* (the sensate) and those of creating the *satva-lok,* (conscious beings).

Self-Styled Sovereign, the Judiciary

(Dramatic deliberation on the state of judiciary)

This is in fact an academic deliberation on the functioning and reality of the judicial system prevalent in India post what they euphemistically call the 'Independence' or, literally, the *'Aazaadee'.* Whose Independence was it anyway? For whom? Except for the ruling class? The lawyers first, and then the hooligans of *Chambal.* Nonetheless, the judiciary of the free country turned out to be one step further than its new crop of leaders; they usurped the entire authority from the latter in subtle moves one after the other. In olden epochs, the autocratic *Sultaans* or *Baadshaahs* dispensed justice purely depending upon their whims and fancies, which were incidental to the moods and tantrums of the Sovereign. Historically as well, the Real Sovereign was the one who dispensed justice. The Judiciary in Indian Republic soon realised this and acted.

XXX

'विदेह' रचित हिंदी ग्रंथ

अनपढ़ लिपि (कहानी-संग्रह)

'विदेह' अरविन्द कुमार की आठ हिंदी कहानियों का संकलन! संकलन की पहली कहानी 'अनपढ़ लिपि में ...' जुलाई, 1992 में प्रतिष्ठित हिंदी पत्रिका 'कादंबिनी' में छपी थी। 'सिग्नेचर' भी स्वच्छता के प्रति सरकारी महकमे की विद्रूपात्मक मनोदशा का कड़वा चित्रण है। 'ताकि आप अपने पक्ष में रहें!' नये प्रकार के कर्मचारियों की मानसिकता को इंगित करती है। 'फिर फिर वही लोग' भेड़-बकरियों की तरह दुरुपयोग किये जा रहे जन-समुदाय के विषय में कहानी है। 'अपार्थाइड' : वस्तुतः तो, शक्तिशाली और निर्बल का भेद ही असली रंग-भेद है। 'नया वेद' 'आज़ादी' नाम से वही पारम्परिक पद्धति चतुराई-पूर्वक 'नया संविधान' के नाम से चलाये जाने की पोल-पट्टी खोलती है। 'पहली कमाई' कहानी का आख्यान कल्पना से भी अधिक विस्मयकारी है! 'भगवान को पैसा' समाज और सरकार दोनों ही की धन के प्रति जो दृष्टि है, उस पर तीखा व्यंग्य है।

पाषाण-युग (कहानी-संग्रह)

'विदेह' अरविन्द कुमार की सात हिंदी कहानियों का संकलन! संकलन की पहली कहानी 'ब्लॉक का पेड़' आज के समाज में क्षीण होते हुए आपसी सौहार्द्र, एवं अजनबियों के प्रति बढ़ते अकारण वैमनस्य, को बिंबित करती हुई सच्चाई है। 'मेरी ज्ञाति' भारत में जातियों के हास्यास्पद 'प्रहसन' – फ़ार्स (farce) -- को चित्रित करके इसकी विद्रूपता को व्यंजित करती है। 'हिंदू-मुसलमान' साम्प्रदायिकता के प्रश्न को व्यक्तियों – दो घनिष्ट मित्रों -- के स्तर पर परीक्षण करके देखती है। 'मुर्गबाज' समय की नब्ज पर हाथ रखने की कोशिश है। 'मंदिरों, मस्जिदों, गुरुद्वारों, गिरजाघरों में ...' साम्प्रदायिक कट्टरता की निरर्थकता को व्यंजित करने के लिए है, जो मृत्यु के पर्दे के पीछे कितनी हास्यास्पद बन जाती है! 'ऐ अधर्मी!' आदमी की नश्ल को बदलने की नाहक कोशिश कही जा सकती है। 'राक्षस' इस नये शासन-प्रशासन में व्याप्त

भ्रष्टाचार पर एक व्यंग्यात्मक टिप्पणी है, और बताती है कि राक्षस कोई कपोल-कल्पना नहीं है, बल्कि आज भी एक वास्तविकता है।

निसर्ग (कहानी-संग्रह)

'विदेह' अरविन्द कुमार की सात हिंदी कहानियों का संकलन! संकलन की पहली कहानी 'मुलाक़ात एक बड़े लेखक से' एक बड़े लेखक और एक आम आदमी के जीवन के साम्य और अंतर दोनों को ही उजागर करती है। 'फाड़ी हुई कविता' एक ऐसे पति की व्यथा-कथा है, जो एक कवि एवं साहित्यकार भी है। 'नया साल' में कुछ भी नया नहीं होता, फिर भी सारी दुनिया किस कदर बाबली हुई रहती है। 'हितैषिणी' शादी जैसी संस्थाओं के पाखण्ड, फ़रेब एवं परम्पराओं से चिपकाव की विद्रूपता पर सशक्त प्रहार करती है। 'छोटे-से शरीर में क़ैदी' शिशुमन की विवशता को चित्रित करती है; वह पूरी तरह माँ-बाप की मूर्खताओं पर निर्भर रहने को विवश है। 'निसर्ग' एक रोमांटिक कहानी है। 'टूट-टूटकर गिरते सितारे' दिखाती है कि कैसे समाज अपने ही शिकंजे में फँसा रहकर ही परेशान होता रहता है!

आर्त-गान (कविता-संग्रह)

'वियोगी होगा पहला कवि, आह से उपजा होगा गान

उमड़कर आँखों से चुपचाप, बही होगी कविता अनजान!'

(*सुमित्रा नंदन पंत*)

या

'मा निषाद त्वम् गम: प्रतिष्ठाम् शाश्वती समा:

यत् क्रौंच मिथुनादेकम् त्वम् वधी: काम मोहितम्!'

(*महर्षि वाल्मीकि*)

चाहे तो आदि कवि वाल्मीकि हों, चाहे फिर छायावादी कवि पंत हों, एक बात तो तय है, कि कविता वियोग या विषाद या शोक से उत्सृजित होती है। पहले-पहल की रचनाएँ हैं ये – जीवन के पहले-प्रहर की; अतः बच्चों के उपयुक्त ही हो सकती हैं बाल-कविता! बाल-कविता इसे मैंने फिर भी इसलिए नहीं कहा है, क्योंकि इनमें मुझे कुछ सार भी सन्निहित लगता रहा है; एकदम तो बकवास नहीं ही हैं ये, जैसी कि बाल (अबोध) -कविता की प्रकृति और प्रवृत्ति होती है। ये कविताएँ 1972 से 1976 के काल-खंड में सृजित हैं; और अभी लगभग अर्ध-

शती की परिपक्व दृष्टि से भी परिमार्जित!

काल-क्रंदन (कविता-संग्रह)

जीवन के प्रथम प्रहर की हृदयाभिव्यक्तियों (1972 से 1976 तक) के 'आर्त-गान' के बाद, 1979 से 1990 तक के द्वादश वर्षीय काल-खण्ड में मैंने जो क्रंदन किया था, उसे मैंने कविता कहा; और उन कविताओं का 'काल-रेख' नाम मैंने चुना था; क्योंकि काल की छाती पर 12 वर्षों तक मैं जो घिसटता रहा था, उस लकीर पीटने को 'काल-रेख' कहना ही मुझे रुच रहा था। परन्तु, कुछ काव्यात्मक स्फुरणा के वश, कुछ काल-अंतराल के प्रभाव-वश मैं अब इसे 'काल-क्रंदन' ही कहना अधिक समीचीन समझ रहा हूँ। साहित्य -- और इसीलिए कविता भी -- जीवन के मूल की अर्थात् सत्य की खोज है: सत्य की परख, यथार्थ की परख! इसमें सब कुछ सुनने-सुनाने, गाने-गवाने ही योग्य है, ऐसा दावा मैं नहीं करता। परन्तु, क्या पढ़ने-पढ़ाने योग्य है, और क्या नहीं, इसका निर्णय भी तो मैं नहीं कर सकता; क्योंकि इसका कण-कण मेरा नितांत निजी सच है! इसमें कितना किस और किसी का भी सच प्रस्तुत है, यह निर्णय उन्हीं पर!

अननुभूत काल (कविता-संग्रह)

अब यह तीसरी काव्य-पुस्तक है! एकदम नवीन काल से सम्बंधित! अभी-अभी हो गुजरे बड़े मानवीय हादसे को रेखांकित करती हुई: कोरोना की महा-आपदा! विश्व-आपदा! जो न कभी हुई थी, और आशा एवम् प्रार्थना ही कर सकते हैं, न कभी भविष्य में होगी! एकदम नये रूप में दुनिया को सोचने को मजबूर होना पड़ा: 'ऐसा भी हो सकता है?' बेतहाशा भागम-भाग में लगी दुनिया अचानक रुक-सी गयी; नहीं, रुक ही गयी – शब्दशः। वायुयान रुक गये, रेलयान रुक गये, बसें रुक गयीं, सारे वाहन रुक गये। मंदिर, मस्जिद, गुरुद्वारे और चर्च भी बंद हो गये: परमात्मा के घर थे वे! हैं! मक्का, मदीना बंद हो गये। वेटिकन बंद हो गया। वह चिरंतन अटूट आस्था जो रुकने का नाम नहीं लेती थी, और आए-दिन छोटी-छोटी बातों पर सिर-फुटव्वल को बेताब रहती थी, अचानक अपने को सकपकाता हुआ पाने लगी। क्या वह बस आस्था ही भर थी, दुनियावी प्राणियों को भरमाने के लिए; क्या उसमें कोई पारमार्थिक सार न था? तार्किक मन यह सोचने को विवश हो गया।

इस कोरोना-काल ने बहुत सारे पाखण्ड-मण्डन किये हैं!

अम्बेडकर-स्मृति (नाटिका)

जाति की समस्या भारत देश के लिए भयंकर होती जा रही है। यह जाति ही है जिसके चलते भारत-भूमि आक्रांताओं के समक्ष प्रणत हो गयी थी। कड़वी सच्चाई यह है कि राजनीतिक चतुराई के चलते 'सत्ताधीशों' ने अपने आप को 'ऊँचा' और सत्ता से 'वंचित' जनों को 'नीचा' मानना शुरू कर दिया। 'आज़ादी' के अधकचरे प्रयोग के चलते स्थिति और भी भयावह हो गयी है; 'नीचे लोग' ऊँचे लोगों को गरियाते रहते हैं: उसके लिए वे 'मनु-स्मृति' नाम की किसी पौराणिक पुस्तक को गरियाते रहते हैं, जबकि वास्तविकता यह है कि आधुनिक भारत के 99.99 प्रतिशत लोगों ने उस पुस्तक का पढ़ना तो दूर, नाम तक नहीं सुना है। उधर, नये सत्ताधीशों ने नयी स्मृति लिखकर -- संविधान लिखकर (जिसकी ड्राफ्टिंग समिति के अध्यक्ष होने के नाते अम्बेडकर को श्रेय मिला हुआ है) – पूर्ववर्ती समाज-व्यवस्था एवं अर्थ-व्यवस्था को एक सिरे से नकार और नेस्तनाबूद कर दिया। समाज के बीच इस पर जो बहस चल रही है, उसी का एक छोटा सा नमूना है यह एकांकी!

प्रिय-प्रवास (संकलन, 'हरिऔध' के महाकाव्य का)

'प्रिय-प्रवास' हिंदी -- खड़ी बोली -- का प्रथम महाकाव्य है, जो स्वनाम धन्य महाकवि अयोध्या सिंह उपाध्याय 'हरिऔध' की अमर कृति है। अत्यंत सुमधुर काव्य के रूप में युग-पुरुष श्रीकृष्ण के गोकुल से मथुरा प्रवास और उनके वियोग से व्यथित गोकुल-वासियों की विरह-वेदना का सरस चित्रण इसमें है। वह एक प्रकार से हर प्राणी की वेदना ही है, जो वह उस समय अनुभव करता है जब कोई स्वजन प्रवास हेतु जाता है या प्रयाण करता है, जो कि संसृति का अपरिहार्य लक्षण ही है। आसक्ति, मोह और ममता सब दुःखों का मूल है; जबकि ज्ञान दुःखों से मुक्ति का साधन! इस महा-आख्यान का यही सार अथच् केंद्रीय संदेश समझ में आता है! 'प्रिय-प्रवास' विरह, बिछुड़ने की वेदना, नैसर्गिक प्रेम और विश्व-कल्याण के संदेश का ही महाकाव्यात्मक सरस रूप है। 'विदेह' अरविन्द कुमार ने इस अद्भुत साहित्यिक कृति को पुनर्सकंलित एवं पुनर्मुद्रित करके इसकी एक संक्षिप्त गद्य-कथा भी इसमें प्रस्तुत की है।

प्रार्थना एवं प्राणांश (संकलित प्रेरक काव्यांश)

बहुत ही सरस और सार्थक प्रार्थनाओं एवं प्रेरणादायी काव्यांशों का संचयन है यह! जो न जाने कहाँ-कहाँ से 'विदेह' अरविंद कुमार ने अपनी रुचि अनुकूल संकलित एवं सम्पादित किया है, उन सभी मनीषियों के प्रति हार्दिक आभार व्यक्त करते हुए, जिनकी रचनाएँ और रचनाओं के प्राणांश इसमें संकलित किये गये हैं। जीवन, मृत्यु के वाहन के आगमन की प्रतीक्षा में रत यात्री के कार्य-कलाप और मनोदशा के अतिरिक्त और क्या है! इस प्रतीक्षा में क्या-क्या अनहोनी अनुभूतियाँ नहीं होतीं! इस प्रतीक्षा को कम कष्टकर करने के लिए काव्य-शास्त्र अनुश्रवण की अनुशंसा मनीषियों ने की है। साथ ही, प्रार्थना के माहात्म्य को भी स्वीकारा है।

मनो पुब्बंगमा धम्मा, मनो सेट्ठा मनोमया!'

भगवान बुद्ध ने मन से ही सृजित होता हुआ इस सकल प्रपञ्च को बताया है। अत: मन को शुचि एवं निष्कंप रखकर आप संसार का अनुभव बदल सकते हैं। जब सभी कुछ कल्पित है, तो सबको अपना मत अनुभव जैसा ही लगता है। परन्तु, है वस्तुतः सब कुछ कपोल-कल्पित ही: न इसे सत्य कहने का कोई तात्पर्य है, न असत्य कहने का! बस मन को साधने का साधनभर है प्रार्थना!

महामुनि वाल्मीकि रचित् इतिहास : उत्तरकाण्ड (वाल्मीकि के उत्तरकाण्ड का गद्यांतरित सारांश)

'रामायण' आदिकाव्य है, न केवल भारतवर्ष का, अपितु सकल मानव-समाज का भी। महर्षि वाल्मीकि-कृत यह काव्य-पुस्तक वस्तुतः तत्कालीन इतिहास है: उस राजवंश का, जिसकी कीर्ति हज़ारों वर्ष पश्चात् भी आज तक अक्षुण्ण है। उस राजवंश के तत्कालीन यशस्वी सम्राट 'राम' का इसमें वर्णन है। राम-राज्य की व्यवस्था, जिसका वर्णन ऋषि ने किया है, आज भी शासन-व्यवस्था के हेतु आदर्श मानी जाती है।

लेखक ने संस्कृत के ग्रंथ का मात्र सार रूप यहाँ प्रस्तुत किया है; सब प्रकार की काव्यात्मकता और अतिशयोक्तियों का निवारण करते हुए साथ ही, आलंकारिकता को आधुनिक संदर्भों से जोड़ते हुए ऐतिहासिक-वैज्ञानिक अर्थों में भी विषय को

समझाने का प्रयास किया है।

कितना यह किसको भाता है, यह तो हर व्यक्ति की अपनी-अपनी रुचि और सोच पर निर्भर करेगा; बहरहाल, लेखक ने अपना दृष्टिकोण प्रस्तुत किया है, वह भी इस चिन्ता से कि नयी पीढ़ी अपनी बहुमूल्य विरासत – गौरवशाली इतिहास -- की ओर एकदम ध्यान नहीं दे रही है। उसका एक कारण ग्रंथों का संस्कृत में होना, और दूसरा अत्यधिक प्रतीकात्मक होने के कारण कपोल-कल्पित-सा लगना, भी हो सकता है; उसी कारण का निवारण करने का यह विनीत प्रयास है।

XXX

लेखक-परिचय

'विदेह' अरविन्द कुमार

भारतीय साहित्य की उदात्त पीठिका को आधुनिक संदर्भों से संपृक्त करने वाले सारस्वत साधक एवं विशिष्ट लेखन-शैली के प्रणेता वरिष्ठ साहित्यकार श्री अरविन्द कुमार 'विदेह' का जन्म 6 अप्रैल 1957 ई को उत्तर प्रदेश के गौतमबुद्धनगर जनपद की जेवर तहसील के छोटे-से गाँव 'मारहरा' में हुआ था। आपके माता-पिता की मानव-मूल्यों में गहरी आस्था रही है। सीमित संसाधनों, बल्कि विपन्नता, के बावजूद भी आप सफलता के लाभी हुए। आपने तत्कालीन आगरा विश्वविद्यालय के अलीगढ़ स्थित धर्मसमाज कॉलेज से भौतिक विज्ञान में स्नातकोत्तर उपाधि प्राप्त की है। आप देश के प्रतिष्ठित बैंक – भारतीय स्टेट बैंक – में दीर्घकालीन सेवा प्रदान करने के उपरांत दिसम्बर, 2018 में सहायक महाप्रबंधक के पद से सेवा निवृत्त हुए हैं।

श्री 'विदेह' छात्र-जीवन से ही अत्यंत मेधावी रहे हैं। विज्ञान-संवर्ग के विद्यार्थी होते हुए भी आपकी साहित्य के प्रति गहरी अभिरुचि रही है। साहित्य के प्रति आपका अनुराग इतना प्रबल रहा है कि बैंकिंग सेक्टर में अति व्यस्त जीवन-शैली वाली नौकरी करते हुए भी आप साहित्य और लेखन से अनवरत रूप से जुड़े रहे हैं। उनकी रचनाएँ तत्कालीन 'कादम्बिनी' जैसी लब्ध-प्रतिष्ठ पत्रिकाओं में काफ़ी पहले छप चुकी हैं; और उनके अन्य लेख एवं कविताएँ अन्य हिंदी, अंग्रेज़ी पत्रिकाओं में यदा-कदा छपते रहे हैं। साथ ही, आपने हिंदी एवं अंग्रेजी भाषा के साहित्य का विशद अध्ययन एवं सृजन किया है। संस्कृत एवं पाली भाषा के साहित्य में भी आपकी गहरी अभिरुचि है।

विभिन्न विधाओं में आपने अब तक 27 ग्रंथों का प्रणयन किया है, जिनमें 17 अंग्रेजी एवं 10 हिंदी भाषा में हैं। हिंदी की पुस्तकों में 03 कहानी-संग्रह (अनपढ़ लिपि, पाषाण युग, निसर्ग); 03 कविता-संग्रह (आर्त-गान, काल-क्रन्दन, अननुभूत काल); 01 नाटिका (अम्बेडकर-स्मृति); 01 काव्य-संचयन (प्रार्थना एवं प्राणांश) उल्लेखनीय हैं। इसके अतिरिक्त आपने खड़ी बोली के प्रथम महाकाव्य 'प्रिय-प्रवास' को भी पुनर्संकलित एवं पुनर्मुद्रित किया है; तथा साथ ही, वाल्मीकि रामायण के उत्तरकाण्ड का गद्यांतरण इतिहास के दृष्टिकोण से आपने 'महामुनि वाल्मीकि रचित् इतिहास: रामायण – उत्तरकाण्ड' नामक पुस्तक के रूप में किया है।

अंग्रेजी भाषा में आपकी उपन्यास शृंखला 'Hypocrisy & Reality' है जिसके अब तक 9 खण्ड वह प्रस्तुत कर चुके हैं (Beyond the Pale; Wilderness of Literacy; Advent of Time; Devoid of Shelter; Price of Refuge; Hatred towards Love; Towards the *Yoga*; On the Descent; In the Exile)। इसके अतिरिक्त, 01 Comedietta (*Chambellion*); 01 Short Story collection (Brainy Beasts); 01 Poetry anthology (Bewailing Muse); 01 Drama (Self-styled Sovereign, the Judiciary); पौराणिक ग्रंथ 'शिव-पुराण' के आधुनिक संदर्भों में अध्ययन पर आधारित 01 पुस्तक (Procreation, the Adorable); 2017 के साहित्य नोबेल पुरस्कार विजेता, Kazuo Ishiguro, के प्रथम उपन्यास 'A Pale View of the Hills' पर आधारित 01 समीक्षात्मक ग्रंथ (Nagasaki: Bomb &

Aftermath) हैं।

'विदेह' जितने मौलिक सर्जक हैं उतने ही समर्थ अनुवादक भी हैं। उन्होंने हिंदी के 02 काव्य-संग्रहों – 'निर्विकार' मुकेश के 'हत्यारी सदी में जीवन की खोज', और 'अश्वघोष' ओमप्रकाश शर्मा के 'अदृश्य का यथार्थ' – का काव्यात्मक अनुवाद अंग्रेजी में किया है, जो क्रमश: 'Search for Life' एवं 'Reality of Invisible' के नाम से प्रकाशित हुई हैं।

'विदेह' के व्यक्तित्व का निर्माण घोर विपन्नता और कठोर संघर्षों ने किया है, जिसका प्रभाव उनकी लेखन-शैली पर निर्भीक अभिव्यक्ति और बेवाकी के रूप में देखा जा सकता है। आपके जीवन का अनुभव अत्यन्त व्यापक रहा है। आपने विपन्नता भी भोगी है, और सुख-सुविधा-सम्पन्न अमेरिकी जीवन भी जीया है; साथ ही, अनेक विदेश-यात्राओं का भी आपको अनुभव है।

केवल साहित्य ही नहीं, 'विदेह' की प्रवृत्तियों में ध्यान-साधना, विपश्यना, योग-साधना, प्राकृतिक-जीवन, आरोग्य, शाकाहार, बागवानी, पर्यटन और पैदल भ्रमण भी सम्मिलित हैं।

2024 के हिंदी दिवस पर – 14 सितंबर को – 'विदेह' को 'शुभम् साहित्य, कला एवम् संस्कृति संस्थान' द्वारा उनके सर्वोच्च सम्मान 'शुभम् रत्न' से सम्मानित किया गया।

'विदेह' की पुस्तकें 'Notion Press', Blue Rose One, Amazon और Flipkart पर तीनों ही प्रारूपों – ebooks, paperback एवम् hard cover – में उपलब्ध हैं।

XXX

About the Author

'Videh' Arvind Kumar

An unflinching adorer of the goddess of wisdom, the *Saraswatee,* and the one who has associated the lofty traditions of Indian literature with the present day contexts, and also, an author of an uncanny style of his own, the seasoned litterateur, *'Videh' Arvind Kumar,* was born on 6th of April, 1957, at a hamlet called *'Maar-Haraa'* in *Jewar Tehseel* of *Gautam Buddha Nagar* distt. in UP. His parents were staunch votaries of human values. Despite unbearable financial constraints, rather extreme wretchedness, he overcame the hurdles of existence and succeeded. He is a post-graduate in Physics from D S College, *Aleegarh,* affiliated to the then *Aagaraa* University. He retired as an Asstt General Manager from the esteemed Bank – State Bank of India – after putting in a long as well as illustrious service there.

'Videh' has been meritorious ever since his school days. Despite being a science stream scholar, he has been showing a keen interest in literature all along. His bonding with literature has been so strong that notwithstanding his pursuing such a busy job as Banking, he managed to sustain his love for literature. His works have been published decades back in the then esteemed magazines such as *'Kaadambinee'.* Also, his stray articles and compositions have found place in various magazines and journals now and then. Besides, he has been a voracious reader of literature and other stuff both in *Hindee* and English languages, apart from himself being a prolific writer and a poet. He is also an adorer of the literature in *Sanskrit* and *Pali* languages.

In variegated genre he has

composed as many as 27 books so far, of which, 17 are in English and 10 in *Hindee*. Among the *Hindee* books, there are 03 story anthologies (*Anapadh Lipi; Paashaan Yug; Nisarg*); 03 poetry anthologies (*Aaart Gaan; Kaal Krandan; Ananubhoot Kaal*); 01 drama (*Ambedkar Smriti*); 01 collection of select poetic pieces (*Praarthanaa evam Praanaansh*). Aside of this, he has compiled, commented, edited and got re-published the first epic of the *Khadee Bolee Hindee*, the *Priya Pravaas*; and a book entitled *'Mahaamuni Vaalmeeki Rachit Itihaas: Raamaayan -- Uttar Kaand'* which presents, in succinct prose form, the ancient history of India as narrated in the most ancient epic.

As regards English oeuvre of *'Videh'*, he has so far published 9 volumes of the long fiction series 'Hypocrisy & Reality' (Beyond the Pale; Wilderness of Literacy; Advent of Time; Devoid of Shelter; Price of Refuge; Hatred towards Love; Towards the *Yoga*; On the Descent; In the Exile) with yet more planned to come. Besides, 01 Comedietta (*Chambellion*); 01 Short Story collection (Brainy Beasts); 01 Poetry anthology (Bewailing Muse); 01 Drama (Self-Styled Sovereign, the Judiciary); 01 book based on the study of mythological volume *'Shiva Puraan'* in the present day context (Procreation, the Adorable); 01 commentary book on the first novel – 'A Pale View of the Hills' -- of the 2017 Nobel Literature laureate, Kazuo Ishiguro (Nagasaki: Bomb & Aftermath) are other books.

Not only an original writer as well as thinker, but also, a capable and versatile translator is *'Videh'* inasmuch as he has translated in English free verse form 02 *Hindee* poetry anthologies, viz. *'Hatyaaree Sadee Mein Jeevan Kee Khoj'* of *'Nirvikaar'* Mukesh Kumaar, and *'Adrishya Kaa Yathaarth'* of *'Ashwaghosh'* Omprakaash Sharmaa with the titles of the books being *seriatim* as 'Search for Life' and 'Reality of Invisible'.

The persona of *'Videh'* has been moulded by constant struggles and abject adversities, which have metamorphosed into his style of narration being quite frank as well as bland, if only straightforward.

His experiences of life are multifarious. He has not only suffered the pangs of extreme poverty and adversity in his childhood, but also, enjoyed the comforts and pleasures of the modern world by living in America. Besides, he has visited and toured in various foreign countries, too.

Not only in literature, but also, in exotic pursuits like meditation, spiritual practice, *Vipashyanaa, Yoga* practice, naturopathy, natural living, *Aarogya,* vegetarianism, gardening, tourism and long walks on foot *'Videh'* is equally active.

To add to his laurels, *'Videh'* has been honoured with their highest honour *'Shubham Ratna'* by the institution *'Shubham Saahitya, Kalaa Evan Sanskriti Sansthaan'* on the occasion of *Hindee Divas*, i.e. on 14th September, 2024.

The books of *'Videh'* are available in all the three formats, viz. eBooks, paperbacks and hardcovers from the Notion Press, Blue Rose One, Amazon and the Flipkart.

XXX

Table of Contents